His
CONVENIENT
HUSBAND
the love and sports series

His
CONVENIENT
HUSBAND
the love and sports series

Robin Covington

Entangled Publishing, LLC
2614 South Timberline Road
Suite 109
Fort Collins, CO 80525
Visit our website at www.entangledpublishing.com.

Indulgence is an imprint of Entangled Publishing, LLC.

Edited by Alethea Spiridon
Cover design by Erin Dameron-Hill
Cover art from iStock

Manufactured in the United States of America

First Edition October 2017

For Josh Lanyon and Adrien and Jake.
Thank you for being my first.

Chapter One

Victor Aleksandrov was a walking wet dream.

Isaiah Blackwell let his eyes linger, confident no one would notice in the press of bodies filling the backstage area. Theater crew, ballerinas, and VIP guests milled around in the cavernous space, hemmed in only by the stage mechanics, sound system, and costumes surrounding them in organized chaos. It reminded him of inside the bowels of the Los Angeles stadium during a football game, the noise and activity seemingly random and surprisingly logical at the same time.

The man in the center of activity was like the eye of the storm, cool and collected as everyone else swarmed around him. His dark, wavy hair was still damp from his post-performance shower, and he was dressed in skinny jeans and an oversize black T-shirt that fell off one bare shoulder, his long feet bare and sexy. His stage makeup was gone, but he still wore black eyeliner and a slight gloss on his lips while a gold stud pierced one ear. He wasn't feminine exactly, but he didn't fit into a purely masculine mold, either.

Stephen would have called Victor "fabulous," and he

wouldn't have been wrong.

And it was his gender-bending fabulousness that had Isaiah's son, Evan, vibrating with excitement next to him. The fourteen-year-old had been levitating with excitement since Ian Carmichael had gotten the tickets for them, and he had talked of nothing since. Ballet wasn't Isaiah's thing, but the arts were Evan's, and so they were here with a hundred of Victor's biggest fans. He watched as Evan wedged between the people in front of them, politely trying to get closer to one of his idols.

"I wouldn't think he's your type," Ian murmured next to him, his lips curved in a knowing grin.

"Who?" Isaiah asked, dragging his gaze away from the sexy dancer and concentrating on his best friend and agent. "Victor?"

"Yes, fucking Victor," Ian answered, his British accent accentuating the sarcasm and making even his profanity seem classy. "The guy you've been eye-fucking since we got backstage." He slid a sly glance over to Isaiah and shrugged. "Well, ever since he got onstage, if we're going for total honesty."

Isaiah didn't bother to deny the observation. Ian had been his best friend longer than he'd been his agent, and any argument would just be him denying what they both knew to be true. Victor was…compelling. Isaiah would have had to be blind to miss the building-sized billboards all over Los Angeles with Victor's lithe, muscular, half-naked body sprawled all over them. The first time he'd seen one he'd almost rear-ended the car in front of him, and it had taken fierce concentration in a preseason workout to tamp down the half-mast boner. No, Victor wasn't his usual type at all, but definitely a man whose sexy charisma and smoking hot body ignited his lust and made him unfit for polite company.

But right now, Victor wasn't fit for polite company, either.

"No. No." Victor's heavily accented voice boomed out from the middle of the crowd. His English was perfect but the weight of the Russian accent sometimes made his words hard to understand. But not at this moment. Every word was crystal clear.

"I don't think my speaking out against the human rights violations in my home country reflects poorly on the ballet company. I am lucky enough to be here as a guest principal dancer for a year and I have a way to make my voice heard, and I will take every opportunity to ensure that everyone knows what my country is doing to gay people. Internment. Torture. People just disappearing as if they'd never existed. If I didn't say anything, *that* would reflect poorly on the ballet company."

It wasn't a new speech for anyone who'd been paying attention for the last year. Victor wasn't quiet about what was going on in his homeland, and he wasn't hiding who he was.

It was as if Ian read his mind. "Stephen would say that Victor was 'out and loud.'"

Isaiah grinned at the memory of his late husband, a college professor whose desire for a low-key and quiet life meshed perfectly with his own. They'd never hidden who they were, but they'd never been the guys to walk at the front of the Pride parade.

"Is there any word on his petition for asylum?" Isaiah asked, searching his brain for a memory of any recent updates on his request.

Ian shook his head. "No. His immigration attorney says he should hear soon."

"It has to be a yes. He can't go back after calling them out for the past year."

"And living openly as a gay man," Ian added. "That alone is dangerous."

"I admire him for his passion and his courage," Isaiah

answered, his eyes straying to his son's face. Evan was laser-focused on Victor, everything in his posture and the light in his eyes displaying how much he admired the man. Evan was such a good kid, artistic and open and compassionate. He was a lot like Stephen.

Victor started moving through the crowd, shaking hands with people and posing for a photo when asked. He made each person the focus of his attention, and it was a skill Isaiah could use when dealing with his fans. He loved to play football, but the meet-n-greets were a challenge for him. Terminally shy and introverted was not helpful when you were the wide receiver on a successful NFL team.

"So, you didn't deny the eye-fucking." Ian broke into his thoughts and clearly not dropping the earlier subject. Why Isaiah thought he would drop any subject in the realm of sex—having sex, thinking about sex, planning for sex—Ian had the sex drive of a twenty-year-old even at the age of thirty-six. No commitments for him, just pleasure wherever and whenever he wanted. "Victor is single."

There would have been a time when Isaiah would have answered with a curt "I'm not," but three years had passed since Stephen had died, and he'd had two very casual relationships in the past year. Stephen was still in his heart, but not in his bed.

"Drop it, Ian. We're here for Evan, not to pick up *your* next booty call."

"I'm talking about *your* next booty call, man. Or only booty call," Ian said, nudging him with an elbow. "You don't have to marry the guy. Just meet him for a drink."

"I'm a grown-ass man. I don't need you to fix me up."

"First, I'm telling your mama that you're cursing again…"

"Fuck off."

"Point made so eloquently," Ian said, making sure to lay the British on thick. "Second, you haven't been laid in six months, and you need to rid yourself of the deadly semen backup before the season starts or you'll play for shit and my fifteen percent won't be as big on your next contract negotiation."

"You're fired," Isaiah growled, keeping his voice low and his eyes on his son.

"Like I haven't heard *that* before."

Isaiah ignored his friend, stepping forward as Victor approached his son, his phone at the ready to take the picture Evan had begged for before they'd headed backstage. The dancer was even more beautiful up close, his skin a light gold that looked paler under the stage lights, muscles toned and lean, eyes dark and flashing with life and fun. Their eyes locked, and Isaiah sucked in a breath, noticing that Victor did the same thing, adding a subtle bite of his lower lip to confirm that the attraction was mutual.

Yes, Mr. Aleksandrov was compelling, and Isaiah felt the magnetic pull between them in his gut. Victor was the first to break the moment, turning to Evan with a huge smile.

"Hello, I'm Victor Aleksandrov," he said, holding out his hand for Evan to shake. The boy beamed, stealing a quick glance in Isaiah's direction before fixating on the current object of his artistic obsession.

"I'm Evan Park-Blackwell, and I love your work."

Isaiah bit back a smile at his choice of words and was relieved with the dancer's reaction. "Thank you. Are you an artist too?"

Evan almost melted into a pile of goo at the question and the acknowledgment of his passion.

"I am. I'm into mixed media art right now. Painting, film, and recycled stuff. I'm also thinking about design. I go to a school for the arts," Evan babbled, not letting go of Victor's hand. "I have a show at school soon, and I'm trying to put together this display on the busting of gender roles and what it means to be gay or straight. I'm thinking of mixing up film pieces with clothing and textiles. I don't know. I'm trying everything right now. I don't want to miss what calls out to me. Ya know?"

"I do. Yes. I do," Victor said, leaning down to look right into Evan's eyes. "Dancing calls to me. It's why I never gave up even when it got hard."

"Exactly." Evan turned to look at Isaiah. "I told you. A *calling*."

"You did." He laughed, ignoring Ian's snicker as he raised his phone and tapped the camera app. "Why don't we grab a photo and let Mr. Aleksandrov speak to his other guests?"

"Dad!"

"Yes, *Dad*!" Victor echoed his son's appalled tone, his expression mischievous and challenging in a way that twisted up Isaiah's insides in the good way. He bit back his own smile; flirting with this man would be a useless endeavor and not a good idea in any book.

Isaiah rolled his eyes and lifted his phone, taking a series of shots of the two of them. Some were the usual poses, and then they morphed into a couple of goofy shots, both of them making funny faces at the camera. Evan was having a blast, and Isaiah silently thanked Ian for making this happen.

"Victor." Ian stepped forward, taking over the meeting. "You've met Evan, the coolest kid in L.A., and I'd like to introduce you to his father, Isaiah Blackwell."

"I've seen you play football, Mr. Blackwell," Victor said, extending his hand in greeting. His skin was warm, long fingers wrapping around his own. He held on longer than necessary, his smile wide and teasing, and Isaiah's belly tightened in reaction. His gaze drifted down to his mouth and the full poutiness of his lower lip. "I was glad when Ian said you'd be here tonight. I've wanted to meet you."

Ah, Ian. Isaiah made a mental note to knock him on

his ass later for obviously playing matchmaker when he'd pretended to do this for Evan.

"Well, I'm Evan's godfather, and I'll do whatever I can to make him happy. I live to see the Blackwells happy," Ian replied, his grin not fooling anyone who knew him at all. "What's the point of being your agent and Isaiah's agent if I can't bring you together?"

"Shut up, Ian," Isaiah grumbled, taking back his hand and putting a little more distance between himself and the sexiest man he'd met in a long time. He surprisingly found himself wanting to extend this meeting, but he couldn't help but notice the anxious faces of the other guests around them. "We really should let other people meet Mr. Aleksandrov."

"Victor."

"Isaiah," he said with a smile. "We really should let you go. We can't hog you all night."

"Okay, I'll let you go," Victor answered, his head dipping in acknowledged defeat. He turned to an obviously disappointed Evan. "I'd love to see your work. If I can help with your project, just call Ian. He has my number."

"I'll be happy to arrange a meeting," Ian drawled, his grin wide and eyebrows raised in an "I love it when a plan comes together" kind of waggle. "I'm great at arranging things... meetings." He paused dramatically, as if he'd just thought of what was coming next. All Isaiah knew was that he probably wasn't going to like it. "Why don't you come to the barbecue pool party this weekend at Isaiah's house? I'll be out of town, but I'm sure the more the merrier."

Isaiah shut his eyes briefly, running through the first ten pages of the playbook in his head. Ian was an asshole, but the thought of Victor in a bathing suit went a long way to ease the sting. In fact, the idea of Victor shirtless made his skin flush hot and his heart pound.

"Yes!" He snapped his eyes open at the sound of Evan's

voice, and his vision immediately filled with the ecstatic face of the one person he loved more than anyone on the planet. "Please, Dad!"

"Yeah, please, *Dad*," Ian echoed, his grin unapologetically shit-eating.

Isaiah ignored his former best friend and focused on his son, contemplating the very limited options he had right now.

Who was he kidding? He had only one.

He turned to Victor, who was looking confused but also hopeful. "You should come to our party. It's casual. Just a few friends."

"Are you sure?" Victor asked, his voice hesitant. "I don't want to intrude."

"I'd love for you to come," Isaiah said, shocked at how much he meant it.

Chapter Two

Isaiah Blackwell was living the American dream.

Victor shut the door to his car, taking a moment to steady his nerves and settle the excitement in his belly. The house where Isaiah lived with his son wasn't lavish, not like the huge mansions hidden behind gates that you often saw on television when famous professional athletes were profiled. No, this was a large home, but it was on a neighborhood street with tall trees and kids riding bikes on the sidewalk in the bright sunshine. It wasn't the childhood he'd had, but it was the kind he'd dreamed about.

The rumble of voices and laughter spilled around the side of the house as he walked up the path to the front door and rang the bell. He shuffled the box of cupcakes in his hands, wondering again if he'd chosen the wrong thing to bring to the party. His friend Alan had insisted he needed to bring something and then vetoed alcohol, since this was a family party. As footsteps approached he really hoped he hadn't gotten it wrong.

He'd liked Evan, a bright young man with a passion for

the arts. And he couldn't stop thinking about Isaiah. Quite a pair, those Blackwell men.

The door swung open, and he was face-to-face with the man who'd occupied his thoughts for the past three days. Isaiah was dressed in a bathing suit and tank top, his dark skin and mouthwateringly toned muscles exposed to Victor's eyes for easy ogling. Football kept this man in top condition into his early thirties, and Victor allowed himself one all-encompassing look before he restored eye contact.

"I brought cupcakes," he said, thrusting the box forward with a smile and a groan at just how dumb he must sound. "Thanks again for having me."

"You're welcome. Evan is so excited you agreed to come," Isaiah said, motioning him inside. "I can't guarantee he won't talk your ear off the entire time."

Victor laughed, his eyes adjusting to the interior of the house and picking up again on the southern lilt that coated each of his host's words. It was like honey, and Victor had always had a weakness for sweets.

"Well, as long as he keeps me away from the cupcakes it will be a fair trade. I can't eat any of that stuff while I'm performing."

"Yes, I get that. Same for me when I'm training." Isaiah paused as they moved through the foyer and looked him over. Head to toe and back again, slow and easy. Victor couldn't help but recognize the appreciation he'd also registered at the ballet. It had been enough for him to Google the football star and his sexuality. It had been no surprise to learn that Isaiah was gay and out. Quietly out.

He'd also been married to a college professor who'd been killed by a trucker who'd fallen asleep behind the wheel three years earlier. From the pictures he found, Stephen Park had been a serious-looking guy with blond hair and glasses and a warm smile. Now it was just Isaiah and his adopted son, living in this house where they'd been a family.

Everything about that story proved Isaiah was not his type. A widower. A father. A man who kept a tight hold on his sexuality. But that didn't stop his body from reacting to the scent of sunscreen and natural musk that washed over him when he stood this close to Isaiah.

Dangerous. Isaiah Blackwell was temptation. Worse than sweets.

"Bread is my downfall. Biscuits in general," Isaiah continued, bringing Victor back to the present with his confession and shy smile. "My mama's biscuits in particular."

"I can tell you don't indulge often," Victor said, unable to stifle his obvious flirting. It was harmless, stupid to act like there wasn't attraction heavy in the air between them. But he didn't think through the comment that slid past his lips. "There's no way you'd fit in those tight football pants if you did."

The seconds ticked by in silence, and Victor wondered if he'd misread this entire situation and was two seconds away from getting his ass kicked out the door and onto the front walk. Then Isaiah laughed, not just the brief chuckle he'd allowed so far but a snort and then a belly laugh that shook his entire body, his hot gaze continuing to clash with his own.

"Oh hell, let's get out to the pool before you get me into trouble," Isaiah said, his deep voice rumbling in the open space as they made their way to the backyard.

The house was comfortable, the rooms open to one another and filled with comfortable furniture and the usual things that teenage boys left in their wake: backpacks, sports equipment, and shoes. This space was no different but was also scattered with cameras, tripods, and bags of art supplies. All the signs that an artist lived here.

The living room and kitchen were open and spanned the width of the house; a wall of French doors across the back displayed the patio, yard, and pool. People were everywhere, swimming, eating, and laughing in the California sunshine. The walls inside and every flat surface were covered with photographs of family and friends, some merely clipped to a display board on the wall next to the doors.

Victor paused to look at them. "So raw. The emotions grab you the minute you look at them."

"They're Evan's," Isaiah said, his voice low but warm.

Victor turned to observe him, examining the play of emotions across his handsome face, the dark stubble on his jaw and surrounding his neatly trimmed goatee. Fuck, he was sexy. "You must be so proud."

"I had nothing to do with it. He's one of a kind." A shout of several voices and a splash drew their attention away from each other and back to the party happening outside. With a nod toward the door, Isaiah led them both out into the sunshine.

The beat of music spilling out of speakers washed over him with the heat of the day and the excited cries of welcome from Evan. The teenager dropped the hand of the older woman he was trying to lead through dance steps, ran over to them and grabbed Victor's hand, dragging him back to where he'd just been.

"I'm trying to teach Grandma to do the whip nae nae, and she's awful," Evan explained, while gesturing toward an older woman in a billowy sundress and huge white sunglasses, her dark hair laced with silver.

"I need a hip replacement, not a dance lesson," she complained, trying to wave off her grandson and the other kids.

"You need to learn from a real dancer, Grandma."

"He's a ballet dancer, boy. Not some fool on the YouTube." She pointed at Victor, smiling as she turned the gesture into a motion for him to come close enough for her to squeeze his hand. Victor leaned in to the touch; he'd spent enough time with fake people during his career to enjoy it when it was real, like now. "I'm Esther Blackwell, and we didn't invite you here to teach me a dance lesson."

"I'm Victor Aleksandrov. It's nice to meet you," he replied, pulling her around and spinning her out slowly.

She gasped, giggled, and whooped out loud when he pulled her back to his body and did a little two-step and then spun her out again until he ended it in a low dip. The crowd broke out in applause and catcalls and general whoops from the teenage crowd. A quick glance at Isaiah found him laughing, still holding those damn cupcakes and standing next to a man who looked weirdly familiar.

"Don't waste those moves on me. I've watched you on the news so I know I'm not your type," she said with a smile and side hug as she led him over to her son. "My son's single."

Isaiah moved like he was chasing the ball down the football field, shoved the cupcake box into his mother's hands, and gently nudged her toward the table of nearby food. "Okay, Mama, go put these away for me and stop harassing our guest."

"Don't you tell me what to do, Isaiah Parker Blackwell," she fired back but without any heat to her words.

"Yeah, don't tell her what to do, Isaiah Parker Blackwell," echoed the man standing to his right.

"Shut up." Victor watched as Isaiah punched out with his right hand, nailing the big man in the gut.

The guy looked so familiar, but Victor couldn't place him. It wasn't because he resembled Isaiah; he'd seen his face somewhere before. The guy caught Victor watching and smiled.

"Hey, I'm Isaiah's cousin, Mick Blackwell," he said, pulling a petite woman with glasses and dark brown hair streaked with gold to his side. "This is my wife, Piper."

"It's nice to meet you." He reached out and shook their

hands and then it came to him. No wonder this guy looked so familiar. "I love your movies, man."

"Thanks. We caught your show. You are a fucking badass on that stage." Mick grunted again when Esther came up behind him and whacked him on the back of the head.

"Mick, watch your language with the children here," she said, handing him a bottle of lemonade. "I assumed you don't drink alcohol during dance season. Isaiah doesn't when he's training."

"You're right. I don't." He looked around at the faces around him, ending with a salute to Isaiah and Evan. "Thanks again for inviting me. This is a beautiful home."

"You got a home of your own when you go back, Victor?" Esther asked, her smile warm and her gaze genuinely curious.

"No. I have an apartment provided by the State near the ballet in Moscow. It's nice, but it's nothing like this." In fact, it was a nice place but it was cold. He was never really there and hadn't wanted to be. "I grew up in public housing, and then I lived at the ballet school. So, no home like this."

"I lived in public housing too, until my dads adopted me," Evan added, his eyes moving from Victor to his father with obvious love. Isaiah beamed back at him, and Victor's belly warmed, his heart skipping a beat or two. Temptation. Sweet temptation.

"So, you know how lucky you are to live in such a nice place, yes?" Evan nodded, smiling when his dad nudged him with an elbow.

"Will your family be happy to see you?" Esther pulled his attention back, continuing with her gentle interrogation.

He hesitated, and Isaiah stilled, his eyes filled with concern with whatever Victor had let show on his face. Isaiah opened his mouth to say something, but Victor cut him off. He didn't mind telling his story. All anyone had to do was Google to find out almost everything.

"I don't have any family back in Russia," he said, shaking his head slightly when Esther's face crumbled with concern. That pain was an old one, and he'd buried it with his mother. "My parents died years ago, and I think I have some family in Chechnya, but I don't know them."

"Oh, honey." Esther leaned in again and pulled him into a big hug. She was soft and warm and smelled like sunscreen and cupcake frosting, and he closed his eyes briefly and just enjoyed the sensation of being mothered. It was childish and maudlin, but he indulged himself in the moment. When he opened his eyes, Isaiah was staring at him, his own gaze filled with something a lot like understanding.

"Thank you," Isaiah mouthed silently at him.

Victor shifted, smiling self-consciously when Esther pressed a kiss to the side of his head and ruffled his hair. They didn't break eye contact, that weird connection that had erupted between them at the ballet going strong. It wasn't something he wanted to give up, the strange mix of attraction and understanding.

"Grandma, stop hogging Victor. I want to show him my school project idea," Evan said, tugging on Victor's T-shirt sleeve. Victor dragged his eyes away from Isaiah and over to the young man brimming with excitement. His dark eyes were lit up from within, the passion of doing something you loved mixed with his innocence made him smile. "I was hoping you could help me."

Victor slid a glance over to Isaiah expecting to find him looking at Evan but he was looking at him and the concentration focused on him made his heart stutter. There was heat and awareness and a silent "thank you" that raised goose bumps on his arms even in the heat.

Oh man. Those Blackwell men. Did he really have any other choice?

He smiled at Evan. "Of course. I'd love to."

Chapter Three

"I should apologize for my mother," Isaiah said.

He stole a glance over his shoulder, watching as Victor paused his own task of stacking the leftover utensils to look up at him with confusion. There was a small outdoor kitchen, and they'd spent the last forty-five minutes putting away all of the leftovers from the party. His sexy guest had insisted that he stay and help, and Isaiah hadn't put up much of a protest.

He'd watched all afternoon and into the early evening as Victor hung out with Evan, allowed his mama to baby him like one of her own, and inflated Mick's ego with a discussion of all of his most popular movies. As his cousin pointed out when Isaiah had told him to shut up, he was "a big deal" in Russia.

"In fact, I think I need to apologize for Mick, too." Isaiah chuckled, turning back to the cold bottles and fishing out two lemonades. He kicked the door shut with his foot and popped the tops off both with the under-counter opener, handing one to Victor. "I didn't invite you to be inducted into the Mick Blackwell fan club."

He couldn't help but stare as Victor rose to his feet, all lean muscles and a fluidity that could be possessed by only a dancer. His T-shirt clung to his body with the sweat of their exertion, and Isaiah took advantage of his guest taking a drink from the bottle to let his attention roam down to the bulge outlined by the snug fabric of his bathing suit. Yes, he was thirsty, just not for lemonade.

"I didn't mind. I'm a huge fan." Victor smiled, moving closer to him and leaning against the counter. They were close enough to trade body heat, which did nothing to explain the shiver that raced across his skin when their arms brushed against each other. "I had a great time meeting everyone."

Silence stretched out between them. It wasn't uncomfortable, which was surprising since they maintained eye contact, almost daring the other to break the connection. It wasn't going to be him. Victor was too compelling.

"I never did get to swim," Victor said, nodding toward the pool and placing his bottle on the countertop. He reached down, his long fingers grasping the hem of his T-shirt and pulling it over his head, tossing it onto the counter with his drink. It wasn't anything Isaiah hadn't seen before; Victor's body was exposed during his performances and on the ballet advertising posted all over town, but up close and so much within touchable reach, he had to steady his free hand on the edge of the counter. "Want to join me?"

Isaiah had been out of the game for a while, but he knew a come-on when he heard it. And this was one shot down the field to him like a football on Sunday. It was up to him to catch it or let it fumble.

And Isaiah Blackwell never fumbled.

"Sure," he answered, stripping off his tank top as Victor kicked off his flip-flops, sauntered over to the side of the pool, and executed a perfect dive into the water. The shirt fell out of Isaiah's hand onto the deck when Victor surfaced, the water running over his smooth skin like Isaiah wanted to do with his own fingers.

Jesus. He needed to cool off. But he knew it wasn't going to happen if he joined Victor in that pool.

He considered it for the briefest of seconds and then followed Victor's lead, sliding into the water and heading for the bottom. A brief touch of the bottom for luck and he aimed for the surface, coming up to his guest's laughter very near him. He shook the water out of his face and found him right there, within arm's reach, and looking very fuckable.

"Did you touch the bottom?" Victor asked, his smile wide and nose scrunched up in confusion.

"Yeah." Isaiah blushed a little, embarrassed to be caught doing the childish action. But he wanted to share it with Victor, he wanted them to get to know each other. No rational reason for it except that he was drawn to him. Not just physically, but more. "I used to do it when I was a kid and taking lessons at Mick's house. We'd race to the bottom. Winner got to pick the first Popsicle."

"You guys grew up together?"

"After my dad died, my uncle, Mick's dad who was my father's brother, brought us here from Texas to live. Our place didn't have a pool, but they did, and when Mick got swim lessons so did I."

Victor smiled at that, shifting toward him, treading water. Isaiah let him close the distance, willing to see where this would lead. He didn't know what it was about this man but it was there, undiluted by even the cool water.

"That's cute," Victor said, his hand brushing over Isaiah's side. He expected to tense at the touch, he was so unused to it these days, but the reaction didn't come. Instead he relaxed, leaning in to the touches hidden by the water.

"I'm not cute," he argued lightly, knowing his tone lacked any heat to carry the day.

"Yes, you are," Victor replied, shoving him back with a hand to his chest and then going under the water, surfacing behind him, really close this time. Close enough for their thighs to touch, chest to back. When he spoke, it was a teasing murmur in Isaiah's ear. "Among other things."

Isaiah spun around to face him, his hand finding smooth skin and allowing a lingering brush against a tight six-pack. "Thanks for staying to help clean up."

"Well, everyone was here one minute and then they weren't."

"Yeah, I think Evan broke the sound barrier running out of here to go sleep over at his best friend's house." Isaiah laughed, not missing the brush of Victor's leg against his own. "You were amazing with him. We're close, but I don't always get the artistic thing." He thought about his son for a few moments and made an admission he didn't often share. "I don't always get the wearing dresses or makeup, either, but…"

"But he's your son and you love him and so you try," Victor murmured, his body ebbing in the movement of the pool, moving against Isaiah in a way that only enticed him to reach out and drag him closer. "You're a good father."

"I try."

"So you don't like it when a guy wears makeup?"

This close, he could see the rim of dark eyeliner around Victor's eyes. It was subtle but effective, making his blue eyes appear huge and inviting. Makeup definitely worked on this man.

"Are you fishing for a compliment?" he asked, loving the flush that crept across his companion's cheek. He had to trace it, lifting his hand and trailing a finger across the skin and tangling it up in a wet curl before he'd even realized what he'd done.

Victor let out a puff of surprise, leaning in to the touch as his voice went husky. "From you? Yes. I don't think you give them often, though."

"I don't." He let his free hand drift underwater, hooking behind Victor's thigh and drawing him close, their bodies now working as one to tread the water. "But you're a very beautiful man, no matter what you're wearing."

He let that sink in, loving the way Victor melted into him, wrapping around him with his legs and arms. Their bodies slid against each other, the water making even their hair like silk, and Isaiah didn't miss the sigh that escaped the man when their cocks pressed together. Victor's lips brushed his own, just a hint of skin on skin but full of invitation.

"So are you going to kiss me or not?"

"Fuck yeah," he said and lowered his head, drawing him in closer and sliding his hand to the back of Victor's neck. He didn't need to do it; the man opened his mouth to him and drew him in, urging him to deepen the kiss with his tongue and the tightening of his arms around his neck.

Victor tasted both tart and sweet from the lemonade, his lips soft, the stubble on his cheek deliciously scraping against his own. Isaiah nipped at his lower lip and groaned when a whimper escaped from between Victor's lips. A shift of their bodies and their cocks aligned, the barrier of fabric between them adding extra friction to their bump and grind. Isaiah lost his rhythm of treading water and half laughed, half moaned before dropping his head to bite at the slick skin on his partner's shoulder.

"If you keep that up, we're going to drown," he breathed out, unable to cover up the hitch in his voice when Victor gyrated his hips and coaxed his cock into full erection. "Damn it."

"Do you want me to stop?" Victor asked, his mouth against Isaiah's ear, teeth teasing the sensitive skin of the lobe.

Another slow rub and Isaiah threw a hand out and grabbed the edge of the pool, pulling them toward the shallow end where he could get his footing. Another shimmy of the man wrapped around him like a monkey and he let go of the side and slapped his ass, smiling when he yelped.

"That hurt," Victor complained, leaning back to glare at him, but Isaiah didn't miss the way he pulled in even tighter.

"You liked it," he replied, grateful to feel the bottom of the pool under his feet. He made his way over to the steps and eased himself down to sit on the top step.

Victor didn't deny it, he just settled on his lap, knees to each side of his thighs, hands placed on the lip of the pool. In this position he surrounded Isaiah, filling his field of vision with nothing but wet, sexy, horny man. It was quite a view.

"And *you* like this," Victor said, rubbing his cock against Isaiah's. Nice and slow. Length against length. "And this," he murmured, lowering his head to kiss and nip and lick along Isaiah's jaw and down across his collarbone. "And this."

Victor was limber, fluid, so he could maintain the slow rub-off while bending to lick at a nipple. His tongue was like sandpaper velvet, hot and teasing the nub into a hard peak of nerves that shot jolts of pleasure right down to his balls. Isaiah couldn't help himself, he reached up and wove his fingers into Victor's hair, encouraging him to keep it up.

"Yes, I like that."

Victor hummed in approval against his skin, looking up at him from beneath the fall of his hair partially covering his face. But not his eyes; the blue darkened to navy with his arousal. He kissed his way across Isaiah's chest, pressing a kiss to his chin and then a deeper one onto his mouth. Teeth. Tongues. Wet heat. Heaven.

"What else do you like, Isaiah?"

He ran his hands over his lover's back, over the hard globes of his ass. Over the fabric at first and then underneath the waistband and over the smooth skin hidden there. Victor watched him, eyes hooded, as he slipped his fingers in the crack, caressing the skin in a slow motion until he found the round pucker he was seeking. He rubbed against his hole, loving the way Victor pushed back against his touch, body begging for what he wanted.

"You like my ass?" Victor gasped out as Isaiah pressed in with one finger, rocking past the tight muscle with a rhythmic pressure met with an answering thrust back into the invasion. "Fuck."

Victor's accent thickened over the word as his eyes rolled back and he arched upward, tossing his head back to the bright moon overhead. Isaiah was torn between soaking in the sight and leaning down to kiss along his muscled torso, licking at the dark pink nipples. Temptation to taste was too much to resist, and he discovered that Victor tasted as good as he looked. Salty but sweet, topped with a layer of masculine spice.

Such a fucking treat.

• • •

"Yes. Deeper. Please," Victor begged.

He pushed backward, gasping when Isaiah added another blunt-tipped finger to his channel. The stretch burned, the sting morphing into pleasure that made his hands shake. His hips jutted forward, rubbing his swollen cock against the man sprawled beneath him. The shallow water splashed around them, its cool slap heightening the overload of sensation when it met overheated skin.

"You are so tight," Isaiah murmured against his chest, his free hand circling Victor's neck and drawing him down for a messy kiss of tongues and teeth and need. His fingers curved inside Victor and hit the spot that made him whimper, a soft keening sound that he refused to stifle. He was never a man to hide his pleasure. Noisy and vocal, his lovers always knew how he was feeling. Some didn't like it, but Isaiah loved it, his own groan dark and low as it carried across the water and into the night shadows beyond the lights of the pool. "Fucking let me hear it. I'm making you feel good, and I want it."

Victor cried out into his mouth, panting and struggling to catch his breath as the sensation of his pending orgasm crept along his skin and lit up his nerve endings. Leaning back from the kiss, he balanced himself on Isaiah's thighs and shoved down his bathing suit, exposing his hard erection to the cool of the night for two seconds before he wrapped a hand around himself and started to stroke.

He should go slow, draw this out. He couldn't. Looking down at Isaiah, his dark skin wet and flushed with his own arousal, the fat head of his own cock peeking out above his own bathing suit, was too much. Victor was past a long, lingering fuck. He needed to come, and he needed to do it before he died from the want of it.

"You're going to make me come," he gasped out between his harsh breaths, now riding the fingers slipping in and out of his body.

"You're so beautiful. Show me how gorgeous you are when you come." The words escaped from between Isaiah's gritted teeth.

"Isaiah."

His name was barely recognizable, mixed with Russian curses and flung out with the first jolt of pleasure that rocked Victor's body. He gripped his cock, back bowing and body clenching around Isaiah's fingers as he seized up with his orgasm. White jets of pleasure shot across Isaiah's chest as his body jerked and rocked with the first detonation and the aftershocks. He was frozen, muscles clenched with the rigor of something so goddamn good that it left him shivering and moaning as he slowly came down from the high.

"Damn. Damn," Isaiah chanted beneath him, his dark

eyes locked on Victor's and roiling with the heat that still lingered there. "I've got to—"

His words broke off with a groan when Isaiah shoved down his own suit and gripped his dick and began stroking with a desperation that spurred Victor into action. He slid down into the water, batting away Isaiah's hand and swallowing his erection down to the root.

He moaned, deep and low in his throat. Isaiah tasted of man and chlorine and desire, and Victor devoured him. He loved sucking cock, loved the weight of a man's erection against his tongue, stretching his mouth and filling him up. Isaiah was perfect, hard and smooth as silk as he slid in and out in a rhythm that gave away just how close he was.

"Victor. Jesus. Fuck, yes," Isaiah said, his fingers wrapped in strands of Victor's hair, giving him the leverage he needed to hold him in place and thrust into his mouth.

Pleasure zinged through Victor at the sensation of being used so thoroughly, of being the source of so much pleasure for him. He'd reduced this huge man to a writhing mass of nothing but sensitive nerves, overheated skin, and guttural groans, and he was lightheaded with the power of it.

Victor looked up from where he rested between his muscular thighs, catching Isaiah's eyes and moving up to suckle his cockhead and press his tongue against the sensitive spot just underneath. Isaiah bucked up, thrusting deep into his mouth at the same time his hand slid across his jaw, his fingers trailing against his skin in a tender caress that was in complete contrast to the frenzied movement of his hips.

"Victor." The groan was half plea and half warning on one last desperate thrust, and then Isaiah was coming.

Victor pulled off and jacked him through his orgasm with long pulls and swipes across the sensitive head. Isaiah shot all over his chest, already dark and slick with water and sweat in the moonlight, his lower lip pulled between his teeth in a grimace of pleasure almost near pain.

He'd said that Victor was beautiful, but clearly he'd never looked in the mirror. Isaiah was stunning, mouthwatering, the most delicious temptation with his toned muscles and dark body hair accenting the cut of his pectorals, the arrowed trail down his belly, and surrounding his long, thick cock.

Large hands gripped his biceps and dragged him upward, water splashing around them as Isaiah claimed his mouth in a wet, possessive kiss. Victor opened to him, welcoming the continuation of their connection and the powerful clasp of his arms around him.

The world tilted when Isaiah flipped them over, caging Victor against the side of the pool as he continued to kiss him. On the mouth, the neck, along the jaw. Victor ran his hands down his back, touching as much of him as he could while they both came down from their sexual high. They exchanged words of nonsense, post-orgasm mumblings that devolved into laughter and heavy sighs.

Isaiah rolled off him, flopping noisily beside him and splashing more water outside of the pool than what was in it. He groaned, chuckling deep and low and in a way that made Victor shiver.

"That was…"

"Fuck yeah it was," Victor agreed, stretching out in the water and enjoying the lingering pleasure. "I don't know how long it takes an old guy like you to get it up again, but I'll be ready if you want to go for round two."

"Fuck you."

"That's the idea," Victor said, dodging the smack Isaiah aimed at him and the splash that followed. He froze a little when his large hand landed on his thigh, the caress soft and almost ticklish where it traced a small pattern on his skin. They sat like that for a while, Victor counting the stars that had demanded they be seen in spite of the streetlights all around.

"I don't do this," Isaiah said, his voice barely above a whisper.

"Neither do I." He felt rather than saw Isaiah's look of surprise. "Don't believe everything you read in the papers."

His companion settled back down beside him. "I should know that. I'm sorry."

"It's nothing." He sneaked a glance at him, drinking in his strong profile. "You're a father. I wouldn't expect that you'd be bringing home a different trick every night."

There was a long pause; he could almost see Isaiah gathering his thoughts, and Victor knew what was coming. This guy had a man he'd loved. They'd had a home together. And now he had to raise their son.

"This was fun, but I'm not looking for anything…"

"Anything serious. I got it. No problem. If I had what you have, that would be my first priority as well." He let out a long breath, making sure Isaiah knew it really wasn't an issue. "When I get asylum, I don't know where I'll be. L.A. has a principal dancer spot open, but that's not a guarantee."

"You're leaving Los Angeles?" Isaiah asked, turning to face him this time, his brow creased in confusion. When he was concentrating on things his lower lip stuck out in a little pout, and Victor had to fight the urge to lean over and kiss him. "I guess I assumed that when you got permission to stay, it would be here."

"No. I'll need to go where the job is." He shrugged it off; there were other alligators closer to the boat. "But I'll worry about that when I get asylum status."

"You don't think you will?" Victor shrugged his shoulders again and his companion barreled on. "You can't go back. They'll…"

"It will be bad, very bad for me," he replied, not wanting to dwell on that kind of conversation tonight. If he was going to get only this one time, he wanted to spend it fucking. Not this. "So, no strings. Nothing serious. Does that mean you want me to go?"

He shifted up on one elbow, looking down on Isaiah and trailing his fingers down his torso, in between the hard muscles of his pecs. Isaiah sucked in a quick breath, holding it as Victor's hand trailed down and grazed the top of his bathing suit. Isaiah's cock shifted under the fabric, beginning to lengthen with the arousal spiking up between them.

"If you promise to feed me some of your mother's amazing leftovers, I'll blow you again," he said, letting the proposition settle between them. He wanted another go at this gorgeous man, but he didn't want to overstay his welcome.

In a flash, he was under Isaiah's large body, legs spread to accommodate his huge frame. They rocked against each other, lips joined in a kiss that was more carnal and messy than seductive, but Victor didn't need to be seduced. He was a sure thing. They broke apart on a gasp and Isaiah's grin was slow and sultry as they ground together, dicks already hard between them.

"If you let me fuck your mouth again, I'll make you breakfast in the morning."

He was surprised. He'd expected round two but got an overnight. He wasn't mistaking it for anything more than a one-time invite. Isaiah had been clear about what this wasn't.

"Sounds like a fair trade," he said, insinuating his hand under Isaiah's bathing suit and stroking his hard cock.

There was something about the Blackwell man he couldn't say no to.

Chapter Four

"Isaiah, you're my best mate, right? I need a favor."

Isaiah narrowed his eyes and glared at oncoming cars as he navigated the traffic in Los Angeles. He'd spent the day at his doctor's office having a full physical to ready himself for the coming season. The kickoff of official training wasn't that far away, and he wanted to ensure that the doc would give him a clean bill of health.

"My physical went fine today, Ian. Thanks for asking," he replied, turning at a busy intersection and reluctantly stopping to let a guy pull into a spot on the street in front of a bunch of restaurants and bars. He'd just left one with the team's general manager, and he was ready to go home. "And my dinner with Masiello went fine as well."

"I know that the meeting went fine. It was great, and Masiello called me five minutes after he'd left you at valet parking. They love you. You win football games and keep your name out of the papers and your dick out of strippers," Ian said, his tone a combination of stressed and worried.

If Masiello was happy, then it wasn't about him. "What's

going on?"

"Victor was denied asylum."

Isaiah didn't need a reminder of who Victor was. They'd had an amazing night together, a breakfast cooked by Isaiah, and then another round of blow jobs in the kitchen before he'd left. They'd texted a few times, mostly about the art project Victor was helping Evan with, but some were flirty. Dirty. And very tempting. But they hadn't gotten back together. Not because he didn't want to…but because he did.

Sex he could handle. Getting off was so much more fun when another person was involved, but he didn't want anything emotional. Victor had emotional potential. He didn't know why, but he just knew it. So…no second helpings. He'd loved Stephen. You didn't get struck by lightning twice.

"How's he taking it?" he asked, already sure he knew the answer.

"He's drinking in a bar. Alone," Ian replied. "That's never good."

"No shit." Isaiah resumed driving, glancing at the clock and calculating how long it would take to get home and in bed. "Why are you calling me? Why aren't you headed to the bar?"

"I'm in Miami."

"Why are you in Miami?"

"Making money. Why the fuck else would I be sweating my English ass off in Miami if I wasn't making money?"

Fair point. Ian was a good guy, but nothing distracted him from the green.

"Who are you lying to in Miami?" Isaiah couldn't help teasing.

"Matt Ames and a prominent person you aren't on the list to know about," he said, his accent perfectly suiting the smugness in his tone.

"Matt's already a client."

He huffed out a huge sigh of exasperation and ignored

him. "I need you to go and get Victor out of the bar before the press find him."

"Why me? You have an office full of minions who can go retrieve a drunk client." Isaiah balked; the last thing he wanted to do was to find himself back in Victor's immediate orbit. It wasn't a good idea.

"The minions I would trust to do this are with me in Miami or elsewhere," Ian replied, his tone reverting to the one he used when he knew he was asking for a huge favor but would never repay it, no matter what he said. "You guys hit it off. He trusts you."

"We came several times with each other's dicks in each other's mouths," he answered, knowing that his characterization wasn't really accurate. It had been more than that. He liked Victor, even when they hadn't been getting off. He was fun and easy to talk to. He made him laugh.

"Whatever. You guys hit it off, and you've been ostensibly texting about Evan when I know you really just want to fuck each other again." Isaiah didn't say anything. Ian would know that he'd hit a portion of the truth. "Please. Go get him and pour him into his apartment before the press finds him. I'll owe you. Please."

Isaiah pulled over, sliding into a spot to stew over this turn of events. He could turn down Ian; he'd done it before. But Victor was another question, especially when he knew what this meant for him. He'd merely said that it would be "really bad," but the fear that had passed briefly over his face had been real. Isaiah had almost pulled Victor to him at that moment, wanting nothing more than to protect him from it, but Victor quickly steered it back to sex.

And Isaiah had been willing to go there with him.

But he couldn't do that tonight.

He sighed and signaled to return to traffic. Evan was with his mother for the night, so he didn't have to rush home. "What's the address?"

Chapter Five

He wasn't drunk enough to be hallucinating.

Even if the bar had been crowded, Victor would have known him anywhere. Isaiah was stunning. Even with his face hard and searching, he was beautiful. And when he saw him, his face softened and he smiled. He was goddamn stunning.

"Victor," Isaiah said, sliding onto the barstool next to him. "Hey."

Victor blinked up at him, confusion mixing with the alcohol in his system and making it difficult for him to gather his thoughts.

"What are you doing here?" Victor asked and then paused as understanding flashed through his mind. He'd turned off his phone after his agent had kept calling. Of course, he'd have called his best friend. "Ian sent you."

"Yep. He wanted me to get you back home before the press found you or before you did something really stupid while shit-faced."

Victor shook his head, nudging the shot glass in front of him. He'd planned to get drunk. It hadn't gone as he'd planned, like the rest of his life at the moment. "I've had two, and this is my third. I know I should want to get shit-faced, but I can't. I'm already numb." He smiled self-consciously, hating how the next part was going to sound. "And I didn't want to drink alone."

"I bet." He watched as Isaiah caught the eye of the bartender and signaled for one of what Victor was having. When the glass of clear liquid slid in front of him, he raised it and saluted him. "You're not drinking alone now."

He slammed back the shot and sputtered a little. Victor wasn't sure what he'd been expecting, but it wasn't what he'd gotten.

"Oh shit. I thought this was vodka." He coughed to clear his throat, face a little flushed from the burn of the liquid. "Tequila is not my friend."

"It's nobody's friend, Isaiah. It's the buddy who dares you to do stuff and then makes sure you go first while he films it for YouTube."

"True that."

Now that he had a drinking buddy, Victor picked up his shot and saluted him in return, taking the entire thing down in one gulp. He slammed the glass down on the bar and quirked an eyebrow at Isaiah in a silent question. When he nodded in agreement, Victor signaled for another round, and they waited while the bartender filled the glasses again. They slammed them back with another salute and then settled into silence.

Isaiah shifted on his stool, taking in their surroundings. It was a dive, the kind of place that was on the local cops' regular patrol because they had frequent fliers who took rides down to the station on a semi-continuous basis. He guessed that it wasn't a place where Isaiah would normally go to drink.

"So, why this place?" Isaiah asked, returning his gaze to Victor. He was wearing dress pants and a button-down shirt that hugged his muscles and emphasized the sexy breadth of his shoulders. He forced himself to focus on answering the question and not on the man he hadn't stopped thinking about since their night together.

"My friend Alan has a crush on the bartender. We've been here a lot."

The man in question came back over to them with two more shots and plopped them down. They picked them up and slammed them back, and Victor made a mental note that it would be his last. He wasn't used to drinking like this, and they'd both be sleeping it off in a corner booth at this rate.

He was feeling the tequila, his muscles loose and thoughts a little fuzzy. It was that spot when drinking when everything, good and bad, was felt but you were relaxed enough not to care.

"I'm sorry," Isaiah said, everything about the slouch of his posture transmitting his sorrow at the situation. "I can't believe they said no."

Victor propped his elbows on the bar and ran his fingers through his hair, ending the grasp with a hard tug and a frustrated groan. "I don't think I ever thought they'd say no. I gave all those speeches and rants about all the shit going on over there, and I never thought they'd say no." He rubbed his hand over his face, his palm rasping over his stubble. "I'm a dead man walking. That's what they call it, yes?"

Isaiah nodded, his entire body taut with tension. He opened his mouth to say something and then closed it, shaking his head. "I shouldn't have had those shots."

"I left my mother. Did you know that?" Victor blurted out, not really leaving him time to respond, just plowed on through, his voice rough and tight with his pain. "Where I come from, when you're talented the government comes to get you. They offer you a new life, all the food you could want, and new clothes and a bed to sleep in that you don't have to share with every other person in your family or bugs. You get to be warm in the winter and cold in the summer. All you have to do is give them your life, your talent, and you get a life better than you could ever dream about in your tenement in Chechnya."

His voice broke a little, and he paused, dipping his head and taking deep breaths to calm himself while wiping away the wetness that had gathered on his lashes. Isaiah reached out and laid a hand on his back, offering support. His touch was heavy, comforting, as he trailed it upward, cupping the back of his neck and giving it a gentle squeeze. His mind flashed back to that night at Isaiah's house. Hard kisses. Wet bodies. Soft sighs.

Not something he needed to be thinking about right now. He continued his confession.

"I was tired of being poor and hungry and cold. I went with them. I left my mother and went with them." He lifted his face, and Isaiah's eyes were dark with pain. Victor's pain. "They didn't just want my talent, my dancing; they wanted me to give up everything I was, and I did it."

"You were a kid," Isaiah said. "I'm sure your mother wanted you to have a better life. Any parent who loves their child isn't going to stop them if they have that kind of chance. They just aren't."

Victor remembered his mother's face, streaked with tears but insistent. She'd told him he couldn't say no; she wouldn't allow it. Her profession of love for him was the last thing she'd said as she handed him over to the government representatives. It was the last time he'd called any place home.

"I'm not sorry for what I said, but I don't want to die," he whispered, the confession harder to say than it was to have someone hear it. While his government denied even the existence of the internment camps, there were many reports of men who were taken away and never came back. He didn't want to be one of those men.

"I don't want you to die," Isaiah said, his simple statement causing Victor's heart to soar and break at the same time. "I don't."

Victor leaned to the left and Isaiah met him halfway. Isaiah pressed a soft kiss to his left temple and Victor closed his eyes, reveling in the sensation of being seen and cared for. It was comfort, the real kind. Not the kind found in the bottom of a bottle, and he wanted it from this man. No matter how dangerous a thought that was, he wanted it.

"You are *nothing* like Stephen," Isaiah said after a long pause, his voice low and laced with his own pain. Bringing up his late husband was a surprise, but Victor leaned in even closer to make sure he heard every word. "He was quiet. Couldn't dance at all in spite of lessons. Two left feet." Victor felt more than saw his smile and the melancholy of his tone. "But he was passionate about what he believed. He wasn't a speechmaker, but he was clear on what was right and wrong, and he never wavered. He did what was right, and he stuck by it." He smiled to himself and slid an indecipherable look at Victor. "In that way, you two are *exactly* alike."

"You loved him," Victor said, hoping the spike of jealousy in his chest didn't translate to his tone.

"I did, and he made me a better man. I learned from him, at least I hope I did." Isaiah pulled back from their embrace and signaled the bartender for another shot. Victor watched him drink it down in one gulp and then methodically and slowly turn it over and set it on the counter. He chuckled, turning to look at Victor with eyes dark and determined. "Let's get married."

Victor stared at him, unable to process exactly what he'd just said. "What did you just say?"

"Let's get married. We can go to Vegas and get it done,

then you can't be deported. Problem solved."

"We can't get married. We hardly know each other." And as much as he wanted to know Isaiah better, this was not how he wanted to do it. It was insane. Ridiculous. He eyed his empty shot glass, wondering if he should order another.

"Look, you don't deserve whatever it is that's going to happen to you if you go back there. If we do this, then you're safe." Isaiah met his eyes, making sure that Victor knew what was on offer. "I'm not talking a love match. I'm not even talking about sex. We'd get married and live together to pass scrutiny of anyone who wanted to invalidate it. We can work out the specifics, but it's the best way to keep you here…alive."

Victor's head was spinning, swirling like a tornado, with a million unknown questions. He didn't even know where to start, what to ask first. No, that was a lie. He did know what the most important question was at this moment.

"What about Evan?"

Isaiah smiled warmly at that. "He's like Stephen. He'll understand."

Victor couldn't sit any longer. He stood up from the barstool, pacing a few feet away and thinking over the proposition on the table. It was an arrangement. A kindness extended to a man whose life was on the line. It was insane, but it just might work.

He turned and faced Isaiah. "Let's go to Vegas."

Chapter Six

He was going to kill his mama.

Isaiah climbed out of his car, glaring at the numerous vehicles in the driveway and parked along the street. There was laughter and music coming from the pool area and a large CONGRATULATIONS banner draped across the front of the house. The words were printed in white on a light blue background and surrounded by white doves, wedding bells, and two gold wedding bands.

Fuck.

He slid his gaze over to Victor, who'd also emerged from the car and was staring at the front door. He shoved his sunglasses on top of his head and turned a confused gaze toward Isaiah.

"I thought we were going to keep this low-key."

"My mama's idea of *low-key* and our idea of *low-key* clearly aren't the same thing." He thought back over the phone call he'd had with her just a few short hours ago. The deed had been done by that point, but he'd called her to let her know what had happened and briefly explained why. She'd freaked out, as he'd known she would, but then had calmed down and sniffled her way through his explanation of when they'd be home and what he needed her to do for them.

His instructions had not included organizing a fucking party.

"Let's see what she's done."

Victor joined him on the walk up the driveway, the sun catching the gold of the wedding ring on his left hand. His own digit was heavy with the weight of the metal. He hadn't worn anything on that finger since he'd removed the one Stephen had given him. That hadn't been an easy day, but slipping this one on had been surprisingly so.

Isaiah was waiting for the panic to set in, the "what the fuck have I done" moment to overtake him, but it hadn't come, and he wasn't sure it was going to. They'd boarded a private jet to Vegas, taken an Uber to the clerk's office and gotten a license, stopped to buy two rings at a jewelry store, and then headed to the first wedding chapel they came to on the Strip.

A few words spoken before a man with an unfortunate toupee on his head and they were married and Victor was safe. There was nothing to worry about. This was an arrangement, a transaction between two adults who knew what this wasn't. No love. No real connection beyond the bonds of friendship. Easy.

He looked over at the man he now called husband and caught him staring back.

"Scared?" he asked, scouring Victor's expression for any clue about what he was feeling.

"Not yet," he answered, squaring his shoulders and trying for a smile. It was a valiant effort, and Isaiah reached out with his hand, letting their fingers graze and then tangle together. What little unease he had, ratcheted back when they touched. Victor had that effect on him, and it wasn't a bad thing.

"My mama will put the fear of God in us both," he answered on a chuckle and inserted his key in the lock of the front door. He thought he heard Victor mumble an "oh shit" just as the door slid open.

The rush of loud, agitated voices in their direction made them both take a half step back. His mother led the charge, with Evan, Ian, Mick, and his attorney in tow. It looked like a firing squad coming straight for him, and he had the fleeting thought to cut and run.

"If you even think about leaving me here, I will punch you in the junk and throw your body between us while I run for it," Victor threatened, his grasp tightening on his own hand but his smile softening the threat.

"Well, it didn't take us long to get to the 'or worse' part of this marriage," Isaiah joked, bracing himself for impact as his mother launched herself at him.

She threw her arms around him, hugging him tight. She was crying, not a lot but enough to accent her words with sniffles. Just as soon as she'd grabbed him, she dropped him like a hot potato and dragged Victor close, treating him to the same rough and tender treatment. His husband stared at him over her shoulder, his eyes wide and expression screaming for Isaiah to do something. He shook his head; trying to separate Victor and his mother right now would be like getting between a mama bear and her cub. He'd figure it out sooner or later that he was now one of her boys, whether he liked it or not, and that gave her access to unlimited hugs and the right to butt into every part of his life.

He was lost in thought, so the smack against the back of his head came as a surprise. Isaiah reached up to rub the spot and noticed Victor doing the same. Apparently, they were both the object of her whiplash brand of affection.

"What were you two thinking?" his mama asked, her tone more disappointed than angry and also holding a hint of pride. "Close the door. The whole neighborhood doesn't need to hear our business. Get in the office to discuss this."

They all stepped in line, following her into his office. It was the only place in the house besides the bedrooms where they could close the door and block the discussion from whomever she'd invited. Once they were all inside, he turned to Evan first, pulling him into a huge hug. His boy was getting taller by the minute, his body muscular and strong. He released him enough to look down into his face. The eyeliner was green today and the gloss was clear. They looked good on him.

"Hey, buddy. How mad was Grandma?"

Evan shifted a quick look at her and then leaned in to answer. "She said that she needed to go to prayer meeting and pray to Baby Jesus over your sorry butts."

Ouch. She was pissed.

But honestly, his mom was the least of his worries. She'd get over it. The guy in front of him was his main concern.

"You mad?" he asked his son, hoping that his assumption that he would understand was correct.

Evan shook his head and hugged him tight and then peered around him to smile at Victor. "Nope. I figured you guys had a good reason."

Relief washed over him. "We did."

"Well, then why don't you explain the reasons to me? What in the world were you thinking?" his mother interrupted, her arms crossed in anger and frustration. She bounced her glare between the two of them, and Isaiah opened his mouth to talk his mother off the ledge, but his husband beat him to it.

"He was thinking that he would help me." Victor moved next to him, his hand on Isaiah's lower back. "My asylum petition was denied, and he wanted to help." His hand moved upward to slide around Isaiah's shoulder, bringing them closer. He looked at him, and their gazes collided, a mixture of understanding, fear, connection. When Victor looked at him that way, he knew they'd done the right thing. "He saved my life."

Ian broke the silence. "And now you're in this fake marriage to fool the immigration department?"

"Not fake." Isaiah struggled with how to explain what this was and what it wasn't. He was answering all of them, but he focused on Evan when he answered Ian's question. It was most important for him to get it. "There are many reasons why people get married. I loved your dad and was with him for years before we were even allowed to get married. Being together was about the way we loved each other. The piece of paper is just a thing. It's what's in your heart that matters. This time it's about doing the right thing. We're both committed to this." He looked at Victor who nodded for him to continue, and Isaiah reached over and linked their hands together. "So, it's not fake."

The people in the room got quiet as they processed what he said, and he let them stew in it. They either got it or they didn't.

"Well, welcome to the family, Victor," his mother said, sniffling as she swooped back in for another hug. Victor huffed out a breath of surprise, but hung on for the ride. When she stepped back, she wiped at her eyes and smiled. "I know you've got papers to sign, so I'll go get the cake ready."

"What cake?" he asked, but she was already headed out the door, dragging Evan behind her. He looked at Victor, unable to hide the alarm. "She got a cake?"

"I think your mother completely misunderstood 'low-key,'" Victor said, his smile wry.

His lawyer interrupted them, handing them both a document. "I drew up the papers the way you asked. No entitlement to each other's assets. No entitlement to alimony or support. These are just paper copies of the ones I emailed you on the plane." He pointed at the final pages. "Sign here, and Ian and Mick can be the witnesses."

They scanned the pages. Everything was the same, everything was in place. Isaiah looked at Victor, picking up the pen on the table.

"I'm good. You good?"

"Yeah."

They both signed their copy and then a third, and then stood back while the witnesses added their endorsement to the papers. All done, they watched as the attorney handed them their own documents and shoved the third in a briefcase. A brief word of congratulations and then he was gone.

"I'm going to hit the restroom before we head out to the party," Victor said, reaching out to squeeze Isaiah's before leaving the room. Isaiah watched him go, admiring the graceful arch of his back, the sexy sway of his hips.

His husband was fucking hot, and he couldn't count the number of times he'd resisted the urge to touch and kiss him in the last twenty-four hours. Well, he'd avoided the kissing. Touching was something neither of them could refrain from doing, everything from a brush of the shoulder to the graze of a hand across a lower back; they connected physically and indulged involuntarily. It wouldn't have concerned him at all, except that it could lead to places he didn't want to go if he wasn't careful.

"Holy shit. If that's how you look at him when he has his clothes on, then we'll never get you out of bed once the season starts," Ian said, his tone mocking and eyes mischievous. "I'll need to call the team and tell them you'll be skipping the Super Bowl to blow your hot husband."

Isaiah groaned, knowing that Ian would be the one to bring this up. "I'm sorry. I think *you're* the one who fucked your way through the last two decades."

"Damn straight I did." He grinned and nudged Isaiah in the gut. "I even fucked a professional ballet dancer once, and it was amazing. He was very bendy."

He rolled his eyes, putting an end to this conversation once and for all. "We're not sleeping together."

"Bollocks."

"No, really. This isn't quid pro quo and not what marriage is about. We're going to keep it on a friendship level, make this work for us and for Evan until the government stops breathing down his neck. Sex leads to intimacy and intimacy leads to feelings, and this is not about feelings."

"Sex doesn't have to lead to feelings. I have conducted several experiments on this, and I can assure you that it's true."

"That's because you're a whore."

"Harsh but fair," Ian answered, his blue eyes scouring his face, and Isaiah willed his expression to go blank. This guy knew him well and if he let him examine him too closely, he'd figure out what a huge temptation Victor was for him. And Ian with that information would be relentless in his pursuit to make sure Isaiah gave in.

"Stop it, Ian. I have Evan to raise and my career to focus on. I loved Stephen, and it's enough. I'm helping Victor, and it's enough. Just leave it alone."

Ian eyeballed him, finally giving in with a disgruntled sigh. "So…no sex?

"No." And if he kept saying it, it would eventually become the truth.

Ian sighed again, pulled his sunglasses out of his pocket, and pushed past Isaiah to head back to the pool. "Well, at least there's cake."

Chapter Seven

"Where did Esther find a wedding cake on such short notice?"

Victor stood alongside Isaiah, both of their hands gripping the handle of a long silver knife and hovering it over the cake in question. Positioned by the pool, they smiled for the camera, both acutely aware of everyone staring at them with huge smiles on their faces.

"The same place she found a wedding photographer and a DJ," Isaiah answered through his frozen, picture-pose smile. "My mama is nothing if not resourceful." He chuckled, the deep one that made Victor shiver in the best way possible. "But she's also a master manipulator, and I think she carries pepper spray in her purse, so don't piss her off."

"Good to know." Victor joined him in silent laughter, catching his husband's eye as they shared this moment. His stomach tightened, desire warming him even more than the clear sunshine beating down on them.

Bodies pressed together from shoulder to thigh, they couldn't have fit a sliver of daylight between them, much less the distance he knew they needed to keep. At least the distance Victor needed. Every time they touched, he wanted more.

This was bad. Very bad.

"Okay, now cut the cake and we'll get a couple pics of you feeding a piece to each other," the photographer instructed with a smile. "You can be naughty or nice with it. I'll just keep snapping."

They sliced through the cake and moved it to a plate, both taking a piece and squaring off at each other with teasing smiles.

"Are you going to be nice?" Isaiah asked, his eyes flicking briefly to the cake in his hand.

Victor smiled, adding a sexy lift to his lips. When Isaiah's gaze strayed to his mouth, he knew he had him. "I think you like me best when I'm naughty."

He moved quickly, knowing Isaiah was fast, a trained professional. But he'd caught him off guard with the seductive remark and smashed the cake onto his lips. The icing squished through his fingers at the same time his husband let out a little gasp of shock. Isaiah's reaction was so startling he didn't pay close enough attention to his hand snapping forward to smash the cake into Victor's face and mouth.

Their guests went wild, laughing and clapping at their antics. Victor laughed along with them, wiping cake and icing off his face, licking both off his fingers while Isaiah followed suit. With his goatee, it was a little more difficult and that only made Victor laugh harder.

"You're so going to pay for this," Isaiah growled in warning.

His tone was rough, sounding a lot like it did the night he'd begged Victor to put his mouth on him and swallow him down. He was looming over Victor, his bulk invading his personal space and giving off waves of heat and his own sexy scent. Remembrance and recognition flashed between them, and Victor felt his smile falter and then he was breathing hard, trying to dislodge the weight of attraction sitting on his chest.

"I look forward to it," Victor responded, eyes zeroed in on his delicious mouth and thinking of all the ways he could make him pay.

The crowd around them was still whistling and catcalling, cheering them on enthusiastically. Suddenly, the sound of metal pinging off a glass joined the sound, echoed by another and then two, until everyone who had a glass in their hand was doing it.

"You have to kiss each other, mate," Ian said, his accent making his voice stand out. "It's a rule."

"I think it's a rule," Victor echoed, his mouth suddenly dry, hands shaking a little. This was a bad idea, but he wanted it. Just one little taste.

Isaiah had the same idea; he shuffled forward the short distance between them, his own desire emblazoned across his face.

"I'm kind of a rule follower," he whispered.

"We'll have to work on that," Victor said, his fingers brushing the curve of his husband's hip and then gripping his shirt when Isaiah lowered his head and swiped a gentle kiss across his lips.

They both stopped breathing for a moment, gazes locked, before they both moved to step away from each other. But their guests weren't satisfied.

"That's not a kiss."

"Make it count."

Isaiah's eyes were dark, his heartbeat pounding so hard Victor felt it where his hand still rested against his body. He was going to kiss him, and Victor knew this was his last chance to stop the madness.

He leaned over and closed the distance himself, covering Isaiah's mouth with his own. His husband tasted of sweet cake and even sweeter icing and underneath, his own special brand of delicious. One dip of his tongue inside wasn't enough so he angled his head and dove back in for more, groaning when Isaiah's hand circled the back of his neck and held him in place. It was hot and wet, and not appropriate for the public or company, but neither of them seemed to care.

Victor wrapped both arms around his husband's torso and held on tight, letting go only when they both had to come up for air. They separated, eyes drifting to the smiling crowd around them and then back to each other.

He wouldn't call the look on Isaiah's face regret, but it wasn't unmitigated joy, either. He was pretty sure his own expression looked the same.

"I think I have icing in my hair," he said, running his fingers through the sticky mess as he backed away. "I'm just going to take care of it."

He turned and headed for the house, waving off Esther's offer to help as he walked on by. He smiled at people he didn't know, escaping to the powder room for a place to think. His friend Alan appeared at his side; his eyebrow rose in a knowing look as he shoved him inside and shut the door.

"I thought you told me this marriage was to keep you in the country."

"I can't believe you didn't warn me about the party," Victor said, glaring at his friend as he tried to get to the sink.

"Ian called me and warned me that Esther would have my balls if I told you, and I like my balls more than I like you," Alan answered, his smile communicating how much he loved being in on the secret. "So, you didn't answer me. I thought this marriage was a fake. That kiss was *not* fake."

"It is," Victor answered, nudging him out of the way to turn on the tap and let the water run until it was warm. He located the icing in his hair and started the process of removing it, using the motions as a cover to hide behind. Alan

Yang was nothing but relentless, and Victor had no answers. "That kiss was…"

"That kiss was fucking hot," Alan said, leaning against the edge of the vanity, arms crossed over his chest. "Your husband is fucking hot. If you screw him as much as I would, then I'm a shoo-in to get your spot as principal dancer, because you won't be able to walk, much less dance."

"Just shut up, Alan," he said, both hands flat as he leaned on the counter staring at his reflection. His lips were slightly swollen from the kiss, the tingling aftershocks still lingering on his skin. "That was all for show."

"I've had threesomes in a sauna that didn't generate that kind of heat."

"Nice visual, but that isn't what's going on here." He slid a glance over at his friend, silently urging him to drop it. "We're not going to be sleeping together."

Alan watched him for a long moment and then placed his drink on the counter, grabbed a towel, and turned the water back on. He reached out, working on a particular spot where he'd clearly missed some of the icing. Victor let him, catching his breath and shoring up his defenses to deal with his husband.

This was going to be harder than he thought. If Isaiah had just been a great body and a big dick, then it wouldn't be a problem. But he was a good son, a great father, and the worst thing of all…a really nice guy. That was his downfall.

"Oh hell, you like him," Alan said, his expression making it clear that he understood the problem.

"He helped me. He probably saved my life," he argued, trying to deflect. It did no good to dwell on the fact that he wanted it to be more than that, that he would be willing to take a chance with Isaiah. That he was the first guy who made him feel that way.

"So, this is all about gratitude?"

"Yep."

Alan patted him on the shoulder before he opened the door to leave. "You keep telling yourself that, and eventually you'll believe it."

• • •

"Alan brought some of your things to the house while we were gone."

Victor followed Isaiah into the master suite on the second floor of the house, the room where they'd spent the night together. It was still the same, all clean lines and dark furniture. Masculine but also attractive, with just enough softness to not make it austere. He tossed his overnight bag onto the bed and followed Isaiah into the adjoining bathroom and walk-in closet.

The space was huge, large enough for a whirlpool tub big enough for an NFL player to stretch and relax tired muscles and walk-in shower so massive it didn't have doors, just a glass partition shielding the room from any overspray from the multiple showerheads. The closet was also in the same space, and when he peered in he found many of his clothes hanging in there on the side opposite Isaiah's stuff.

He turned and faced his husband, giving him the first direct look of the evening since their icing-smeared kiss of earlier. The guests were gone, and Evan was ensconced in his room, and now it was just the two of them working out this marriage so nobody got hurt.

"So…" He let the silence spiral out between them. It wasn't awkward, but saying the wrong thing could make it that way. "Evan seemed to take it well."

Isaiah nodded, leaning back against the opposite doorframe. Even though it was wide, they dwarfed the space, two big men trying to occupy the same space. They'd have to get used to it.

"He was the least of my worries. He's a good kid and understands what's going on in this world. Growing up poor and biracial in the system, he gets that life isn't a puzzle easily solved. Add in two daddies and he had to grow up fast. Luckily, he's got a great heart and is way smarter than his old man."

"You're doing a great job with him."

"It wasn't me. It was all Stephen, and I'm trying not to screw it up."

The mention of his late husband turned the tone of the conversation. It wasn't awkward, but it wasn't the easy relationship they normally had. Standing in the middle of the house where they'd built a life, in the room where his clothes had hung next to Isaiah's, drove home just what an imposter he was.

The shift of mood signaled to Victor how difficult this was going to be. What had looked simple in black and white wasn't going to be easy to navigate. They could all be hurt if this went badly. He was already interested more than he should be. His body was all in, and it wouldn't take much for his heart to join. He was a romantic, unapologetically so, and it was a miracle he'd never really fallen for anyone before. He'd had crushes, but they'd burned out as quickly as the sweat had dried on their bodies.

But there was something about Isaiah that triggered thoughts of sweaty nights between the sheets and a life built together in a home filled with love. It didn't take years of therapy to figure out that Victor was searching for the things he didn't have as a kid: a home, security, love. He wanted those things, and it was only natural that his mind would drift to having them with a guy he had a connection with.

A guy like the one standing in front of him now, eating him alive with eyes that strayed to his mouth and lingered. Victor's heart hammered in his chest almost to the point of being painful. The desire between them was always there, just waiting for a spark, and apparently one look from Isaiah was all it took.

Victor took a step forward, but his movement broke the spell between them, and his husband shifted back, retreating from the closet and to the bathroom beyond.

"So, the sleeping arrangements…" he began, clearing his throat and flexing his hands in an uncharacteristically nervous gesture. Isaiah was normally such a confident man the gesture stood out. But if there was anything to be nervous about, working out sleeping arrangements with the man you just married but barely knew was one that qualified. "I know we need to put up appearances for any government people who might want to challenge the marriage…"

"But we don't want to force our family and friends to lie all the time, either." They'd discussed this on the plane, knowing all of it was going to be tricky.

"Exactly. This suite is ideal for this. We'll have to share the bathroom, but we'll both have our own space." He waved a hand toward the bedroom where they'd been. "You'll have that room and I'll be in here."

That got Victor's attention. Their previous night together they'd spent in Isaiah's room, and he just assumed that they would carry on in the same way. Victor watched as his husband moved to the door opposite the bedroom and opened it.

He followed Isaiah through the door, taking in the room before him in one comprehensive glance. It was a bedroom, its warmth and welcoming feeling the opposite of the other. This was a lived-in space, full of favorite objects and special items lining the built-in bookcases and every flat surface in sight.

The area rug covering the hardwood floors was plush under Victor's bare feet, and the scent of Isaiah's cologne wrapped around him. The linens on the bed were rumpled, and discarded clothes were draped over the leather armchair in the corner. Isaiah, Stephen, Evan, and Esther were the main subjects in the photographs, their faces shining out from every size and shape of frame.

This was where Isaiah slept. Where he had spent nights with the man he loved and made a home with.

This was not the place where he'd spent the night with Victor and where he would spend every night.

That was the guest room.

The lurch in his stomach was unreasonable, stupid even. But it didn't stop it from hurting anyway.

He'd been a fool.

And nothing made that clearer than Stephen Park-Blackwell's face smiling out at him from the table right next to where Isaiah laid his head. It was the last thing Isaiah saw when he went to bed and the first thing he woke up to in the morning.

Isaiah had been clear that this was never going to be anything more than an arrangement of convenience and friendship. No sex. No emotions.

His husband was already married in any way it counted, and Victor needed to remember that, if he had any chance of making it out of this with his heart intact.

Chapter Eight

"Let me congratulate you on your marriage."

Isaiah shook the hand Mr. Glenn Masiello extended out to him when he reached the table in his favorite restaurant. The smaller man had a firm grip and a big smile, something that made him approachable to the players and staff on the team. People ran into trouble only when they underestimated him because of his friendly demeanor and ended up on the wrong side of the bull's horns. Masiello was a fierce general manager and an exacting taskmaster. He expected his team to win games and keep their noses clean.

Isaiah had been a performer on the field, and he'd been a married man with a kid, not anything the tabloids would want to print. So his dealings with the guy had always been pleasant, but something about the urgency of this meeting made him uncomfortable.

"Thank you, sir. I appreciate it," he answered, seating himself and giving his drink order to the waiter standing by.

They spent the next few moments perusing the menus and making their choices, the only conversation about the specials and whether a substitution could be made on a particular dish. Small talk that ran until the waiter returned with their beverages and then left with their meal orders in hand. With a few moments to themselves, the boss wasted no time getting to the point.

"I have to say that we were all surprised to hear of your marriage." He chuckled, taking a sip of his wine. "And in Vegas no less. If you'll forgive me for saying so, it doesn't seem like your speed. Totally unexpected."

That was the understatement of the century. Nothing about what had happened had been cookie-cutter Isaiah Blackwell, especially the attraction that had bloomed between the two of them. When he was around Victor it was impossible to keep his eyes off him, and he'd barely managed to maintain physical distance. Married life had been surprisingly no-stress and fun with the beautiful man, with nights at home and easy conversation. If Victor sometimes withdrew during times when they were alone, Isaiah chalked it up to his respect of their ground rules. And while Isaiah wanted to throw the damn "no sex" parameters out the window, he was grateful he wasn't struggling with that part all by himself.

Cold showers had become his best friend lately, especially when Victor ran around the house half naked. There was only so much a mortal man could take. But his lunch companion wasn't interested in his sex life…or lack of one.

"Well, there's nothing about Victor that is expected," he said, unsure about where this conversation was going. Victor wasn't a guy who needed someone racing to his rescue, but Isaiah wasn't going to let someone trash talk him, either. No matter the reason they got married, he was his husband, and he would defend him if necessary.

"Yes. Yes." Masiello pondered his glass of wine, fiddling with the stem while he took a moment to collect his thoughts. The delay from a man who often made quick decisions told him that the probability of his not liking where this was going was high. "Victor is quite a vocal advocate for the LGBTQ causes."

"Well, he's gay, so they would be very important to him." Isaiah took a deep breath and steadied his temper. It would do him no good to jump to conclusions about what Masiello really meant.

"Oh, and we are also staunch supporters of LGBTQ rights and all of our employees who fall into that category," Masiello said, his hand pressed outward in a gesture of commiseration. "Don't get me wrong, I'm not criticizing him. He's been admirably outspoken about the situation in Chechnya and elsewhere. Quite a force to be reckoned with."

"Then what are you saying? I'm not following."

"Isaiah, you've never hidden who you are or your relationship with Stephen, and I would never ask you to. In fact, I'd fire anyone who dared to do so."

"But…" Isaiah prompted, irritated that he wasn't just getting to the fucking point.

"But this sport isn't easy for a gay man. I'm not telling you anything you don't know. Other players, fans, sponsors, and advertisers, many of them feel like they get to have a say in how you live your life. I know you've had to put up with harassment and discrimination in your career, and it's truly admirable that you've persevered."

"I appreciate your support, but I don't understand what Victor's activism has to do with me."

"He's your husband."

"And we didn't mind-meld when we said 'I do.' I support his advocacy and would never think to stop him from doing what he needs to do, but that doesn't mean that I'm suddenly going to change who I am." He took a deep breath and steadied his voice, making his final point as concisely and clearly as he could. "I'm the same man who's played football for you for the last eight years. I'm a private man, and I intend to keep it that way."

"I just hope your husband has the same outlook, because I don't know how it would fall out if things suddenly changed for you."

Isaiah blinked, now really confused. "I think you need to explain that last statement."

"Quite simply, the franchise really doesn't like our players' personal lives to negatively impact the team. It doesn't matter if it's the wife or husband of a player, we'd like our team members to avoid public controversies that could be divisive among our fans and advertisers. We want the focus to be on football and not what's printed on the front page of the newspaper."

And there it was, finally clear. They didn't want any trouble of the gay or straight variety. They wanted to make sure his makeup-wearing, Pride-parade-marching husband wasn't going to upset the macho fan base. Message delivered loud and clear.

The funny thing was that Victor was the most respectful and well-spoken advocate out there on the subject of human rights violations against LGBTQ people. He dealt in facts and never got dragged into the ugliness when the press and haters tried to bait him. Yes, his level of living "out and proud" made Isaiah uncomfortable, but they were working it out. The only thing Isaiah had a fast rule about was keeping Evan out of the line of fire. He was too young, and he deserved his privacy. So far, it had been fine, and he expected nothing different in the future.

"Mr. Masiello, my husband is more vocal than I am, but I can assure you that his advocacy isn't going to adversely impact the team. And while I fully support him, I won't be joining him on his platform."

Isaiah stared across the table at his boss, hoping that this would be the one and only conversation they'd have about this. He had no idea how Victor would react if he told him he needed to cool it on the activism front. It wouldn't go over well. In fact, if they had been having sex, he'd definitely be sleeping alone in the guest room. Or in the doghouse…if they had a dog.

Masiello smiled, reaching for his wineglass to give Isaiah a salute. "Glad to hear it. I knew I could count on you."

Isaiah smiled back, hoping that he could count on his husband.

• • •

"How is marriage going?"

Victor looked up from where he was shoving gross dance clothes into his duffel bag to see his best friend approaching from the practice areas. Sweaty and panting, Alan's shit-eating grin was way too bright for someone who'd just spent hours working on a new dance performance.

"It's fine, Alan," he responded, zipping up the bag. "We're getting along great."

"Oh yeah." The guy plopped down next to him on the bench, and his grin got even wider. "Is the sex amazing?"

Victor did a double take. "I didn't say anything about sex."

"Well, that's a fucking shame." Alan scowled, twisting off the cap to his water bottle and taking a huge gulp. His grin was gone, eyebrows screwed together with concern, and Victor braced himself for a conversation he didn't think he was going to enjoy. "Seriously, Vic, the heat between you two was combustible. What are you waiting for?"

He dumped his duffel on the floor and slumped down on the bench, letting the feelings he normally indulged only in the privacy of his room wash over him. It was stupid. Ungrateful. All he could think about sometimes.

"We're sleeping in separate rooms. He's in his bedroom, the one he shared with Stephen, and I'm in the bedroom he created for Evan just after Stephen died. It had been a study, and when Evan was having trouble sleeping he converted it into a bedroom." He licked his lips, wondering for the millionth time why the next part always hurt him. "I'm in the room where we spent our night together."

"Oh man, that's rough."

"I don't know why it bothers me. It was a hookup."

"A fucking mind-blowing hookup."

"Yes, it was that, but it was also more. Or I thought it was." He sighed, thinking back over the months since he'd met Isaiah. He'd clearly blown "getting blown" out of proportion. "I just misread the entire thing. It was stupid, and I'm just glad everything is working out."

"So, the married part of being married…"

"It's really great. It's the three of us, four when Esther comes around, and we've got a routine. It's nice and normal, and the first stable thing I've had in a long time. I don't want to do anything to risk it."

"Vic, what could you do to risk it?" Alan laid a hand on his arm, giving him a reassuring squeeze. He could be an asshole nine-tenths of the time, but when he was a good friend, he was a good one. "Look, I'm not going to give you the speech about how you deserve to be happy, blah, blah, blah. But you're a good guy and what you want…the home and family? That's not out of your reach, not with the right guy."

He'd thought maybe Isaiah had a chance to be that guy.

"I've got that now. In a way. I'm going to be satisfied with what I have." Victor stood, lifting his duffel bag off the floor and slinging it over his shoulder. "I need to go. It's my turn to make dinner."

Alan raised an eyebrow. "Watch out. The next thing you'll be having family game night with root beer floats."

"That's on Thursday nights," he said with a smile and headed home.

Chapter Nine

"Dad, Victor is cooking again."

Isaiah tossed his keys into the bowl on the table in the foyer, looking up the stairs to where his son leaned over the railing. His hair was in long dreads, and he was wearing a dress. Isaiah didn't mind the dress, but he couldn't quite wrap his mind around the dreads. Instead of hanging down, they stood out all over his head, and he resembled Medusa on the losing end of a fight with a light socket.

Not that he would say anything. A word from him might be laughed off or kick off days of sullen teenage angst. The only person whose comments were always taken with a smile were Victor's. His husband could do no wrong as far as Evan was concerned. He was smitten along with his mama and Mick and even the cynical Ian.

And if he were honest, just like him.

"Dad, did you hear me? Victor's cooking again."

The clang of pots and pans from the kitchen punctuated his announcement, and Isaiah groaned a little on the inside. It wasn't that his husband was a bad cook, he was just a messy one. And not just the garden-variety type of messy. After Victor was done they needed to hire an industrial-strength cleaning crew to make the kitchen habitable.

He followed the noise, cringing when something metal hit the tile floor. So far, Victor hadn't broken anything, but it was still early days. When he rounded the corner and walked into the combined family room and kitchen, the sun highlighted the carnage, and in the middle was the most beautiful man he knew.

His husband was shirtless, pale skin gleaming with a slight sheen of sweat as he lifted the pasta insert out of a pan of steaming water and placed it in the sink to drain. His muscles flexed under taut skin, the dark hair in his pits and down his treasure trail highlighting his breathtaking masculinity. He was wearing Isaiah's favorite pair of sweatpants, formfitting and low-slung on his hips.

Everything about him ignited a hunger in Isaiah's gut.

Victor looked up and caught Isaiah staring, his smile softening his look of concentration as it rolled out at a sensual pace. That look was something he'd begun to look forward to seeing at the end of the day.

Just like he loved the way reminders of Victor had sprouted up all over the house. His dance bag on the floor of the entryway with Evan's backpack and his practice gear, his copies of *People* magazine and *Scientific American* on the coffee table, episodes of cooking shows on the DVR, and the scent of his expensive cologne lingering on the pillows on the couch.

Victor was part of his life. An unexpectedly welcome change for a man who wasn't looking for it.

"Hey, how was the meeting with Masiello?" Victor asked as he placed a bowl of salad on the dinner table.

"Can I help?" Isaiah asked, waiting for directions. Victor was like his mama when he was cooking—you didn't enter the vicinity or touch anything without explicit permission.

"Yes, please. Take the bread to the table, and tell me about your meeting."

Isaiah picked up the basket, lifting the cloth to smell the warm garlic bread, covering it back up when Victor glared at him. He was cute when he tried to boss him around—not something he'd confess, but it wasn't the first time it had crossed his mind.

Evan joined them and in the unspoken communication he was developing with his son, Victor motioned for him to take the sauce to the table while he transferred the pasta to a serving plate. It smelled delicious. The aroma of garlic and tomatoes and something spicy filled the air, and his stomach growled in reaction. But the best part of the entire scene was watching the two of them together.

Victor was great with Evan, and it shouldn't have been sexy as hell, but it was.

"This smells awesome, Victor. Thanks!" Evan crooned after a gulping inhale of the delicious scents drifting up from the table. His eyes rolled back in his head with exaggeration. "You make the best pasta ever."

Victor laughed. It was almost a giggle. "You're welcome. When I first lived on my own I had very little money, and pasta was cheap and filling. I tried every kind of sauce, and some of them truly sucked."

"You didn't have to cook when you were younger? Did you have chores?"

"No, not really. My job was to dance. The staff at the home took care of us."

Isaiah perked up at his mention of the home. Victor didn't mention his childhood often and usually only the information that would be revealed by a Google search.

"Were there other kids at the home?" Evan asked, setting cutlery at each place. "Did you have lots of friends there?"

"There were other kids, other dancers, and I had some friends, but the 'home' wasn't a home, not like what you have here." Victor paused, considering Evan for a moment, and then threw an arm around Isaiah's son. His expression was softer, his eyes kind, and Isaiah's chest ached at the scene before him. "I don't know what you remember about being in the system…"

"Some people were nice. Some weren't. I just never knew how long I was staying…" Evan answered, his voice a little hoarse with obvious sadness.

"So you didn't want to think about it as home." Victor finished his sentence with what Isaiah knew was personal experience. You couldn't fake the connection the two of them had. Just like he couldn't fake the connection with Victor. Or deny it. "It was the same for me. I knew that I was there only because of my talent. If I got hurt or couldn't keep up, I was gone. So, I never allowed myself to get too comfortable. I never thought of it as home."

"I never got comfortable until my dads brought me home."

"That's good. You got good ones. A great family," Victor said, giving Evan a squeeze and a smile.

Victor moved to let him go, but Evan hung on, his smile tentative and his words sweet. "You've got us, too. Right?"

Victor paused, swallowing hard before turning to look at Isaiah. Isaiah couldn't miss the shadow of some other person pass over his face. It was that kid, the one who'd grown up in a home with no family, who still wanted it.

He turned back to Evan and nodded. "Right." Another squeeze and he nudged him toward the counter. "Go grab the pitcher of lemonade."

Victor swiveled back toward Isaiah, his smile wide. He gestured at Evan with both hands and then clasped them over his heart.

Yeah. Evan got you like that.

But he wasn't the only one.

Isaiah moved close to his husband, reaching out to trail his fingers down his arm, their fingers briefly tangling while he smiled back at Victor, silently mouthing "thank you" before Evan returned with the pitcher and plopped it down on the table. They stared at each other for a few seconds, the air crackling with the spark between them but also the heaviness of a deeper connection. He dropped his hand, needing the space of even a few inches. For not the first time, Isaiah wondered if he'd offered to marry Victor because of the Stephen-shaped hole in the middle of this family. Not that Victor would be a perfect fit, but he could take up some of the space. Isaiah knew he'd been selfish to offer, especially when he kept his heart closed off and there was no chance he'd let Victor try to repair the damage.

Breaking eye contact when Evan declared that he was starving, they settled around the table, passing the dishes and catching up on the day. It was a scene he'd come to love since he'd married Victor a few weeks ago. Any doubts he had about their being able to make this work disappeared in moments like this.

It was only when they were alone that he was worried this would fail, because he couldn't manage to keep his hands off him. And if he put his hands on him, he just might fall for him, and that wasn't something he could handle. Not again.

Victor made it hard to stick to the rules.

"So, tell me how the lunch went with Masiello," Victor asked him as they ate.

"It was interesting. He congratulated me on getting married," he said, making sure he relayed the rest of the conversation in the way he'd practiced in his head. Isaiah didn't want to piss off Victor. "He wanted to remind me that the franchise values my skills on the field and the fact that I keep out of the tabloids."

He let that statement stand on its own, unsure of whether Victor would let it lie. His husband wasn't exactly a "let it go" type, so he wasn't surprised when he spoke up.

"And what did he have to say about the fact that your spouse has a harder time staying out of the papers?"

"He said…" Isaiah suddenly forgot everything he'd planned in the car on the way home. He looked up at Victor, helplessly motioning that he had no answer to the question.

"Let me guess, the franchise would prefer your husband be less…out?" Victor's face was serene, but he wasn't fooled. He was hurt or pissed, or maybe a combination of the two. It was hard to tell when he put on his performance face, becoming whatever the moment called for. It was fascinating and intriguing and maddening.

"You can't change who you are," Evan said between huge bites of pasta. "You're gay. So's my dad. Everybody is different."

"Masiello isn't asking Victor to change. He's just asking for us to be careful about not letting the press print bad stories about us."

Victor considered this, twirling spaghetti on his fork. His jaw was tight, but he lifted his eyes and met Isaiah's gaze across the table. Everything in his posture and the fire in his eyes told him that he wasn't going to back down.

"I can't control the press coverage, Isaiah," he said, his voice as tight as the grip he had on his utensil. "I don't want to cause trouble with your boss, but I can't back off this subject. It's too important. And if I get to sit pretty here in the United States, safe and free, I can't be silent." He hesitated for a moment and then shook his head, his posture relaxing but his expression registering more frustration. "Not that your job isn't important. It is."

"I'm proud of what you're doing." Isaiah glanced at Evan,

including him in the praise. "We both are, and I'm not asking you to change anything about it. If we keep on like we have, we'll be fine. Okay?"

Victor paused for a moment, before nodding. "Okay."

"Is it still okay for me to come to the ballet and film the rehearsal on Wednesday?" Evan asked, his enthusiasm dispelling the lingering awkwardness of the moment. "Emma and Cauldon are still coming with me if that's okay."

Victor smiled, the one he had just for Evan, and nodded. "Sure. I arranged it with everyone, and it's fine. You can't interrupt what we're doing, but you can film it for your project."

"That is so cool! My project is going to be the best in the entire class, and I'll be a shoo-in to get the spot in the visual arts program. They never give it to a sophomore, but I think I've got a shot."

"If passion and excitement and hard work mean anything, I'm sure you'll get it," Victor assured him. "When I was your age I won a role that everyone wanted. I was the youngest dancer to ever audition, and so many people told me I couldn't."

"But you did it anyway."

"I did, and I proved them all wrong," he answered, smiling at him with a look that made Isaiah clench his hands in his lap to keep from reaching out and touching him. Victor was sexy in his own right, but when he showed love for Evan and went out of his way to help and encourage him, it made resistance so difficult to maintain. "You do your best, you give it everything you've got, and if you don't get it, you keep trying. Keep coming back so often that they don't have a choice but to give you the chance to succeed. Talent is important, but tenacity is key. Nobody ever got anywhere by letting people tell them no. Your dad will agree with me."

"I've never been the fastest or the strongest player. I was

just the guy who wouldn't quit. Not on myself, not on my team." He smiled at Victor in agreement. "He's right. Make them work to ignore you and tell you no. They won't be able to do it."

"May I be excused to call Emma?" Evan asked, his ass half off the seat with excitement. He'd inhaled his dinner in typical teenage-boy fashion, and to keep him here would be cruel.

"Sure. But come back down in fifteen minutes because you've got cleanup detail," Isaiah said.

"Sorry," Victor said with a grimace.

"No problem!" Evan yelled and took off for his room, his steps pounding up the stairs two at a time.

He looked at Victor and they both laughed when his door slammed overhead, his excited chatter to one of his best friends preceding the boom.

"You're good with him. Thank you."

"He's an easy kid to love and help. You've done a good job," Victor said, leaning back in his chair and settling in for a chat. It was what they did—have dinner and then talk about their day. It was nice, fulfilling, and addictive. Lately, Isaiah had caught himself doing and thinking of things he wanted to remember to talk to Victor about later.

It wasn't something he thought about too much. It was too…revealing about what he was feeling for his husband.

"It wasn't me. It was Stephen," he answered, thinking of how much Stephen would have liked Victor, how he'd be here telling him to jump in with both feet and see where things could lead. Stephen hadn't been fearless, but he knew a good, calculated risk when he saw it, and he'd make sure he didn't miss it.

"You always say that," Victor murmured, his voice low and face partially in shadow as the sun went down outside the window. "So, tell me about Stephen."

Chapter Ten

There were a million different kinds of silence.

Awkward. Intimidating. Easy. Tense.

This one was heavy. With importance. With revelation. With the closeness that was developing between the two of them despite how hard Victor tried to keep an emotional distance. Every night he went to bed a short distance from the room where Isaiah had lived and loved Stephen, and he told himself it was okay. They were friends, a family of sorts, and he had no reason to envy a dead man.

Well, that wasn't entirely true.

But he constantly had a feeling he was living with a ghost; the memory of Stephen was everywhere. Not just in the photographs displayed all over the house, but in the air they breathed. He could have sworn he caught glimpses of his smile on Evan's face, felt the warmth of his personality in the comfortable furnishings he'd chosen, and his presence in the lingering scent of his cologne in the closet.

But he'd never heard about him from the man who still mourned him.

"Did I ever tell you about how I met him?" Isaiah asked, nodding when Victor shook his head. He nodded again, as if he was prodding himself to disclose this part of his history, to share something he wouldn't get back if he let it go. Victor waited, unwilling to push if he wasn't ready, but hoping that he was.

The silence stretched out so long that Victor rose to his feet, gathering their plates and taking them over to the sink. Isaiah was an active man, and his conversation followed the lead of his body; if he were moving, he would talk. If he were seated, he'd lapse into quiet observation. So, if Victor wanted him to talk, this was the best way to get him to open up. When Isaiah joined him at the counter, bowls in hand, Victor knew he'd tell him what he wanted to know.

"I was in my first year of playing for the NFL and the PR department signed me up for one of those awful bachelor auctions for charity. I was out, but it didn't seem to matter. So, I was there getting raffled off like no black man should, and vowing I would never do it again, and I saw a man in the audience with glasses and the world's worst haircut and a scowl on his face that would make anybody think twice about approaching him in a dark alley. When the winning bid was declared he walked away, and I couldn't find him in the crowd."

"He was the winning bid," Victor said, thinking this was like those romance movies on TV where the first meeting of the couple was the kind of thing that never really happens in real life. *Of course* this would be the way that Isaiah met Stephen, because by every account their love story was epic. He was surprised when Isaiah continued and shattered all of his assumptions.

"No. He didn't win; he couldn't afford the opening bid on a college professor's salary, and he was pissed. When I caught glimpses of him throughout the night, he was always scowling, and his hair was sticking up all over because he kept running his hands through it in frustration."

Isaiah brought the last of the dishes over and placed them on the counter, leaning against it to finish the story. He was clearly lost in the past, his eyes unfocused and lips curved in a hint of a smile. Isaiah in love was a gorgeous sight, and Victor couldn't help but move closer. "At the end of the night, just as the band announced it would be the last song, he walked over to me and asked me to dance. It came out more like a demand, because he admitted later that he was afraid he'd chicken out."

"But you don't dance," Victor said, remembering a specific conversation about how Isaiah didn't dance if he could help it.

He chuckled, low and deep, and Victor felt the wave of jealousy wash over him at the sound. It was ridiculous, but real.

"There was no way I was telling him no. Stephen was…" He paused to consider his words, shaking his head when he couldn't find the right one. "We danced this thing called a bachata. It's from the Dominican Republic and he was taking ballroom dance in his spare time so that he didn't spend all his time in a lab. It was slow and sexy, and I couldn't take my eyes off him as I followed his lead. We left the party together, and that was pretty much it. We were just together after that night."

"The bachata is a gorgeous dance. Very sensual." Victor considered what he knew about the man. "The scientist had a romantic side."

"He did. His brain was always full of formulas and numbers, but when he focused on me…" Isaiah swallowed hard, his emotions making his voice steel wool rough. "When he focused on me, it was like I was the only person in the world."

Victor didn't even think. If he had thought about it, he

would have talked himself out of it, but his body took over, and before he knew it he'd pulled Isaiah into his arms. Nothing sexual, nothing calculated, just an embrace for a man who'd lost something precious and who'd carried the weight of his grief, and the grief of his son, on his shoulders.

Isaiah didn't fight him, just melted against him, his large arms wrapping around Victor's body as he allowed the moment to spool out naturally. Victor slowly released the breath he was holding, afraid that any sudden movement would spook Isaiah back into his previous arm's length regimentation.

The house was quiet, soft music drifting out from the docking station, Evan's muffled footfalls overhead as he undoubtedly chattered away with his best friend. He curbed his desire to make this more than it was, ignoring the voice in his head that whispered that this was what he always thought having a family would be like. A warm, safe home, children, and a man who loved him, and building a life together.

This wasn't it, but it was as close to perfect as he was likely to get, so he'd take it. For as long as he could have it. They'd never discussed an end, but the natural end date was when he gained his citizenship. So, three years. Not long, but he'd take it, because Isaiah was quickly getting to him, taking up residence in the part of his heart he'd never thought would be filled.

Pathetic? He didn't care. Victor was a romantic, something he had in common with Stephen. And look how Stephen had fallen. Victor didn't have a chance.

The music switched, shifting down into a slower rhythm, not a Latin beat by any measure, but sultry. They began to move together. Victor didn't make a conscious decision to dance, but it was the language that came most easily to him, and he responded to the natural sway of the embrace.

Isaiah followed his lead, the shuffle of their feet falling

easily into a modified variation of the bachata. Limbs pressed against each other, muscles flexing as they moved slowly, finding their own pace. Victor sucked in a breath when Isaiah's hands ran across the bare skin of his back, callouses dragging and igniting sparks of arousal in their wake. He made a sound, low but audible, and somewhere between a gasp and a moan, prompting his husband to pull back, eyes locked on his own.

Victor was relieved when he didn't end the exquisite torture, but instead continued to maintain eye contact as they swayed together in the honey-glazed light of the kitchen. He was hard, sure that Isaiah could feel it through the thin material of his sweatpants, because he felt Isaiah's erection through his dress pants. They shifted against each other, cocks aligning in a way that made the most of the lazy friction, sending ripples of pleasure over his skin and up his spine.

And then Isaiah pulled him closer, and Victor buried his face in the sweet dip of his shoulder, inhaling the scent of laundry detergent, cologne, and the intoxicating smell of his man. Isaiah's hands dipped lower on his back, fingertips skimming the waistband, the occasional slip below the edge ratcheting his heartbeat up to the point where he knew it could be felt by the man holding him.

"So beautiful." The words coasted across Victor's skin, barely above a whisper. "Such a temptation."

"I'm here for the taking," Victor replied, his fingers coasting over the nape of Isaiah's neck just to satisfy the urge to feel skin.

The moment was cloaked in madness, which was the only explanation for his mistake, and he knew it was the last thing he should have said when Isaiah went still, his fingers unconsciously digging into Victor's hips.

They both pulled back, slowly, stubbled cheek against stubbled cheek, until their mouths were touching. Victor licked against his husband's soft lips, begging for entrance and diving in when he was granted admission. Spice and sweet lemon and heat were everything in this kiss, more exploration than demand as they held on to each other and gave in.

The remains of dinner were around them, but this was another kind of hunger, and he'd waited too long to have it satisfied. Victor knew how good they could be together, and while he knew they would walk the razor's edge between emotion and pure physical indulgence, he was willing to risk it. If he fell, then he'd embrace it.

But he knew he'd be falling alone.

Isaiah's large hands cupped his ass, lifting Victor against his body and rotating their hips in a slow, arousing motion. They both moaned, Victor clutching Isaiah's shoulders, pulling him closer. He wanted no daylight between them, wanted his husband inside him, filling up all the spaces.

The slam of the door above them broke the moment, both of them registering the progress of Evan downstairs and neither wanting him to walk in on this. They both stepped back, and he felt every inch of distance emerging between them. They pulled away. If Victor couldn't explain to himself, he couldn't explain to his stepson.

Isaiah was breathing heavily, his chest rising and falling as he adjusted his length in his pants. Victor looked down; the obvious tenting and a spreading wet spot would be impossible to hide in these pants. He looked up at Isaiah, catching him staring at the same spot, tongue dipping outside to slide along his swollen bottom lip.

"Isaiah," Victor murmured, whatever he intended to say dying in his throat at the look of desire and guilt on Isaiah's face.

"That's...we can't do that," Isaiah said, his words definitive, but his tone uncertain. "That would be a bad idea for us."

"There's something between us, Isaiah. So much that

avoiding it has become a full-time job." Victor shuffled closer to his husband, using their physical attraction to what he hoped was his advantage. It was probably all kinds of wrong to try to entice this man away from a decision that he'd clearly thought out, but…Victor didn't mind being wrong. "Would it be such a bad thing?"

"I can't give you more than that."

"Do you think you can't move on? That you can't live?" Victor knew he was treading into dangerous territory, but he couldn't help it. He didn't understand, and he was tired of flying blind.

"I don't want to, Victor. I've had love and everything that goes with it, and I don't want it." Isaiah's voice was gaining conviction as he strove to make his point before Evan made his way back into the kitchen. "Sleeping together would be the first step to a place I don't want to go."

Victor had no answer to that. He wasn't going to beg for something Isaiah didn't want to give.

"Victor, I don't expect you to be alone. Just be discreet."

Victor barely controlled the swift exhale of breath that threatened to escape with that emotional sucker punch to the gut.

"What?" he asked, hoping that he'd misunderstood.

Isaiah licked his lips, his discomfort obvious. "You can take lovers…other men. Just not here at the house, and be discreet. It wouldn't be good for it to get out."

Victor wished he hadn't asked. The truth didn't make him feel any better.

It didn't matter that his husband's entire demeanor screamed that he wanted this to be different, that he wanted them to be more. Maybe it was the knowledge that they could have something, if Isaiah let it happen, that made this… permission…impossible to take.

Or maybe it was because he realized that at this moment

he'd crossed the line from "I could fall" to "tumbling head over heels." He could lie to himself all he wanted, but the painful clench in his chest called him out.

"Hey, I'm here to clean up," Evan said, his dreads bouncing and bobbing with each of his steps. Powered by excitement and teenage levels of energy, he was oblivious to the emotional standoff happening between the adults.

Taking advantage of his entrance, Victor removed his arm from Isaiah's grip and moved out of the room. The steps, mounted two at a time, and short jog down the hall had him in his room and behind the privacy of a closed door before Isaiah could stop him.

Sliding his sweatpants over his thighs, he let them fall to the floor and padded over to the bathroom, entering the walk-in shower and turning on all the taps. The water was hot, as hot as he could stand it, the wall-mounted full-length showerhead beating his tension and anger into submission. The clear glass of the only other wall caused the sensation that the entire bathroom was the shower, and Victor had to admit that it was his favorite part of this suite. Normally a shower in the gorgeous space would fix all the day's aches, inside and out. But not now. He was still tense, taut with frustration and unspent desire.

He really had no right to be mad at Isaiah. They'd never discussed having an open relationship, and Victor had never contemplated having sex with only his right hand for the next three years. He'd stupidly thought Isaiah would change his mind, that they'd have more of what they both clearly enjoyed during their one night together.

Fool. Dreamer. Idiot.

Victor looked at his reflection in the mirror across the room, not liking the whipped puppy expression on his face. Turning his back on his pitiful self, he squirted shower gel on his hand and started soaping up. Pits and chest were covered in suds and then lower across his abdomen to his cock and balls. He was still hard, the impact of Isaiah's kiss and his anger keeping his body ready for release.

What the hell. He wasn't going to get it anywhere else tonight, and he refused to slide between his sheets aching and wanting.

Victor turned, leaning against the lukewarm tile of the back shower wall, staring at his reflection. He gripped his dick, firm and tight the way he liked it most, watching the pink head slide out of the foreskin on the downstroke. He moved his hips, mimicking the thrust of his hips if he were fucking a wet, willing mouth.

Isaiah's mouth. Full lips pulled back and throat open to swallow him down.

Victor wouldn't let Isaiah touch himself. This was punishment, after all, penance for making him wait, for hurting him, even intentionally.

His husband's large, dark-skinned body would be in submission at his feet. Isaiah's long, thick dick would be hard, flat against his belly and pulsing with its need to be touched. He would moan around Victor's cock, chasing it with his mouth on the retreat, hands clenched in desperation on his muscular thighs.

Victor would tease, rubbing the head along the lips, allowing only quick tastes of what Isaiah wanted so badly. And then, when he was on the verge of coming, Victor would reach out and cup the back of his head, thrusting fast and deep into his pretty mouth, letting go only when Isaiah opened his eyes and gazed up at him.

Victor groaned, shoving his dick into his fist and opening his eyes to find the real Isaiah staring back at him in the mirror. Not fully inside the bathroom, partially hidden by the door, playing voyeur in his own home. Isaiah's swift gasp told Victor he knew he'd been caught, but he made no move to go away or join him. Anger flared again and mixed with desire, and he was on the edge.

If his husband wanted a show, he'd give him one.

"Isaiah," Victor moaned out loud, the anguished sound ricocheting around the room as he came. He fucked his fist, riding the exquisite pleasure erupting in his belly and racing across all his nerves, ending with sparks of fire in his nerve endings. He kept his eyes open and locked on his husband until the last ripple ebbed away and he slumped against the wall on legs whose muscles had turned to mush.

Isaiah didn't move, but his chest heaved and he bit his bottom lip. Victor waited, unwilling to guess at what would happen next. He was tired and too bruised from the last encounter to be the one to make the next move. The next play was all on Isaiah.

The water ran tepid, and he shivered, shifting slightly to turn off the flow, and when his gaze returned to the mirror, Isaiah was gone.

He had his answer.

Chapter Eleven

"The last time I looked at a guy like that I considered popping the question."

Isaiah slid a glance over to Ian, who'd taken the seat to his left in the rehearsal room for the Los Angeles Ballet, but he didn't hold his attention for long. On the floor, dancers of both genders and almost every ethnicity leaped and dipped and soared across the space, executing moves that would be helpful to know on the football field. If he could catch air like Victor and his friend Alan, there wouldn't be a player on the field who could catch him.

Evan and his friends were following them, close but not intrusive as they took video footage and still photography for Evan's project. All the dancers were amazing, but his eyes kept straying to his husband, thirsting over the ripple of his muscles and the bulge in his practice gear. His cock was half hard, just begging him for a little attention…preferably from Victor.

Isaiah threw another glance at Ian, making sure this one made it clear he wasn't biting at whatever hook he was tossing in the water. He was too tired to keep up with Ian's witty British banter today.

"Yep, I'd marry him," Ian said, his tone light, teasing, and wrapped up with a hint of naïveté. Isaiah wasn't fooled. The last time Ian had been innocent Magic Johnson was still playing basketball, and Mick's dad had taken them to see him play in one of his final games. Ian continued with a big smile and a slap against Isaiah's arm. "Oh, but you already did!"

Isaiah rolled his eyes, using distraction and deflection to keep Ian away from the topic he didn't want to talk about. "The great Ian Carmichael almost took a walk down the aisle? Why didn't you marry the guy?"

"It wasn't love; it was just a great blow job. See, he did this thing with the bottom part of his tongue…" Ian flexed his tongue, making a gesture that Isaiah hoped he never had to see again.

"Stop. Stop. Nobody needs to see that." He pushed at Ian, breaking out into a chuckle he now realized was the point all along. This is what made them friends—Ian knew when he needed a shove to get the fuck out of his head.

They both faced forward again, watching the scene unfolding on the dance floor. Victor was amazing, his entire body under his complete control as he flexed and jumped and snapped to attention exactly on the beat of the music. Anybody who didn't think a dancer was an athlete was fooling themselves. He knew for a fact that Victor's two-a-day workouts rivaled any of the ones they did at the football stadium and that many of his teammates wouldn't be able to keep up.

The only downside to his fitness was the fact that his husband loved to walk around the house shirtless, wearing the tiniest and tightest of shorts. It was heaven and hell all wrapped up in a tight-assed, delicious package.

"He's magnificent," Ian murmured, as if he could read his

mind. "You know, there are worse things than falling for the guy you married who also adores your kid."

Isaiah sighed. Ian wasn't wrong. "I know."

"And a satellite couldn't miss the gigantic 'but' hanging over your head." Ian let that settle between them as they watched Evan and his friends moving between the dancers to get footage from every angle. "Is it because of Stephen?" Isaiah shook his head, but his friend kept going. "I knew him, man, and at the risk of sounding like Dr. Phil, I don't think he'd want you to be alone."

"It's not that." Isaiah knew what the problem was, but whether he should say it at all was the issue, because if he gave it voice, then it would be out there, and it would be true. "I don't want to go through that again."

Ian knew. He always knew. "Being hurt? Losing someone?"

"Yeah. When Stephen died, only Evan kept me from going with him. I don't ever want to go through that again."

Ian whistled under his breath. "Victor must have really gotten under your skin if you're worried about losing him so much that you won't let yourself have him."

Isaiah's brain was screaming in warning, and every muscle in his body tensed. He wasn't ready for this conversation after all. "I told him I wasn't expecting him to be celibate. I asked only that he be discreet."

He left out the part where he'd followed him, desperate to say something to erase the look of hurt and pain on Victor's face, and stumbled into his favorite fantasy and worst nightmare. Victor, wet and naked and hard, fucking into his own hand. The sounds he'd made were debauched, dirty, and depraved, and Isaiah had barely fought off the urge to join him, to drop to his knees and take him to the back of his throat. When their eyes had met in the mirror… Well, what scared him most was the surge of emotion in his chest that overshadowed the ache in his groin. He'd run like a coward and jerked off in the hallway bathroom, grinding his teeth together to bite back his own shout of release.

This morning had been...odd. Victor acted completely normal, except he failed to sustain eye contact. In fact, all contact, physical and otherwise, had ceased, and Isaiah missed it. Craved it.

He felt, rather than saw, Ian turn to him, his words ripping him out of his memory. "You're a son-of-a-bitch, Isaiah Blackwell."

"Why? Because I told the truth? This isn't a real marriage. I did him a favor making it clear he had permission. Three years of blue balls could be deadly."

"I take it back. You're a fool. Something much worse," Ian said, his shoulders set in a stiff clutch of anger. "We'll talk again when you realize your man is on his knees for somebody else and you want to drown yourself in your pool."

Isaiah really didn't understand his reaction. Ian was not the settle-down-and-have-babies type, and normally not one to push his buddies into the "holy state of marital hit-or-miss," as he liked to call it. But that was something he didn't want to unpack today, so he opted to switch the conversation to one that always grabbed Ian's attention.

"The meeting with Masiello went fine. He wanted to congratulate me and make sure Victor wasn't going to put us on the front page with his activism."

"Victor's position on the human rights violations in Chechnya aren't going to damage the club, and he's an idiot if he thinks so. I hope you didn't agree to something stupid and likely discriminatory and in violation of your contract." Ian stood with him as the rehearsal broke up, dancers and teenagers scattering in all directions. Victor was talking with his friend Alan and Evan, looking into the viewfinder of the camera, presumably at the footage they'd just shot. "Let's gather your men and get something to eat. I do have serious business to talk to you about."

"You mean you've been working instead of busting my chops?" They moved across the floor, drawing closer to Evan and Victor.

"Fuck you. I'll tell Matt Ames to ask someone else." Ah, the name of his friend and former Olympic athlete piqued his interest. Ever since starting his own athletic clothing and performance gear company, Matt had been hinting at a business proposition, and it looked like he had moved on to the action phase of his super-secret project.

"Anything Matt needs, I'm in." Isaiah half turned to face Ian, pointing in his smug face. "Just make sure I make money. I've got a kid who's going to be an artist and will probably be living with me the rest of his life."

"Oh, you're hilarious."

"I am." Victor turned, and their gazes clashed for an instant before his husband dipped his head and rubbed his face with a towel. Isaiah turned his focus back to the kid who was his whole world. Flushed with excitement and grinning from ear to ear, Evan made him smile. This young man was his life. The rest was…superfluous. "Did you get what you needed?"

"Holy crap, Dad! I got everything! This was…" Evan jumped up and hugged Victor, causing the man to stumble back a couple of steps before he stabilized them both and squeezed him back, Victor's face morphing into pure happiness. "Thank you, Victor."

"Yes, thank you, Victor," Isaiah said, noting that his husband didn't respond to his comment, just focused on Evan and his own excitement.

Ian had said it wouldn't be so bad if he fell for a man who also adored his kid. He wasn't wrong, but Isaiah just… couldn't.

Evan was back, gripping his arm and dragging him toward the exit. "I have to get home and edit this stuff. I am going to kill it!"

Isaiah glanced toward Victor, eyebrow raised in inquiry. He hadn't showered yet and might not want to get into a car with the remains of four hours of practice all over his skin.

"I'm good. I can shower at the house." Victor answered the unspoken question, tossing his towel into the receptacle on the stage and pulled a T-shirt over his head, covering up his miles of pale skin and ripped muscle. When his head emerged, he caught Isaiah staring, but the usual heat was replaced with a chilled distance and then a rapid break in connection. Isaiah had never felt so completely shut out in his life, and he didn't like it, but discussing it with an audience wasn't going to happen. They had to figure out a way to make this work if they were going to last peacefully for three years.

"Let's go."

They followed Victor through the warren of halls and tunnels in the building, past racks of costumes and props and equipment. They emerged into the employee parking lot, the sun beating down on them from the cloudless blue sky. Summer in California: this was why people stayed even after their dreams died. A bad day in this sunshine was better than a good day anywhere else.

Victor stopped abruptly in front of him, his strong, tall body like a brick wall that caused them all to rock like dominos. Isaiah reached out with no thought to steady but to protect his husband from whatever was ahead of them, causing his entire posture to go rigid.

"Victor! Victor!"

A swarm of reporters pressed forward, their microphones and cameras shoved in their faces. Evan gasped, and Isaiah reached out with one arm, pushing him back behind his body, protecting him from anything that might happen with this group of vultures.

"Victor, what do you say to the reports that the stories of persecution of homosexuals in your native country are made up?"

"Is it true that you're going to testify before Congress in support of gay rights?"

Victor glanced behind him, his head nodding toward where their truck was in the parking lot. "You go ahead with Evan. I'll handle this."

He didn't wait for Isaiah's answer, but he didn't need to—Isaiah was already ushering Evan away from the fray and toward the relative privacy and safety of their vehicle. It was impossible to ignore the shouted questions still ringing out behind them, and he felt, rather than saw, Evan's reaction to one shouted out above the noise of the others.

"So, what do you say to your critics who call you a liar and coward for hiding out here in the United States?"

Before Isaiah knew what was happening, Evan wrenched out of his grasp and was barreling toward the wall of press. He was a growing young man, and sometimes Isaiah could see the man he would become in the breadth of his shoulders and hear it in the timbre of his voice. But now…he just looked like a kid staring down the barrel of a gun.

"Victor isn't a coward or a liar! You don't know anything!"

As soon as Evan spoke, the collective attention shifted, and they moved en masse, focusing in on his son. Fear sliced through him, cold and sharp, and Isaiah took the first step to cutting off what was going down when he spied Victor doing the same. Too little, too late.

He shoved through the crowd, jostling reporters aside with enough force to send a couple of them down to the ground, shouting and spewing venom with every breath. The remaining ones peppered Evan with questions, their equipment shoved in his now alarmed and frightened face.

Victor inserted himself between Evan and the crowd, shoving him toward the truck. "Open it and get in. I've got him."

Isaiah quickly skirted around the back of the vehicle, unlocked it, and slid in just as Victor flung the passenger door open and shoved Evan inside. His son was pale and he looked like he couldn't decide whether to urge them to drive and get away or to push Victor out of the way to take them all on, one by one.

The whole situation amplified the tension he'd carried between his shoulder blades since he'd married an almost stranger and ignited his papa-bear instinct. Isaiah lashed out at the most convenient target: Victor.

"Jesus. What the hell, Victor? Is this your idea of keeping us off the front page? What the hell were you thinking with Evan here?"

His husband turned ashen, except for two red patches high on his cheekbones and the anger lighting up his eyes to blue fire. He leaned into the truck through the open door. "Do you think I'd do this? That I would put him in this position? I can't control where the reporters show up, Isaiah."

"You expect me to believe you didn't know they'd be here? When do you pass up a chance to give a sound bite? All I've asked is that you think about this family, my son. You can't even do that." Isaiah jammed his key into the ignition and started the truck, the rev of the engine mimicking his racing heart. He tried to calm down and not make a scene. There were reporters outside the window, and he knew that they'd bite at whatever story they could get their hands on. A chink in the veil of marital bliss would be a great story. A story his team wouldn't want on the front page. "Just get in the damn truck and let's go."

He knew he'd made a mistake the moment Victor's eyes flashed with what Isaiah now knew was a combination of anger and hurt. And damn, he was tired of being the guy who put that look on his face. He just couldn't seem to help himself.

"No. I'll go back in and get my sound bite," Victor said through gritted teeth and turned on a dime, his long legs eating up the distance to the door. His obvious anger sliced through the crowd of reporters. He was a big man, and they knew that to block him would be a bad idea. The sight of all of them parting like the Red Sea for Moses would have been funny if this wasn't such a shitty situation.

"Go get him," Evan said, his hand on the door handle and body angled to follow his idol and stepdad.

Isaiah reached out and wrapped his hand around his son's forearm, effectively barring him from going anywhere. Evan struggled for a minute and then turned hurt and betrayed eyes on him.

Damn.

This shit was impacting Evan now, and *that* Isaiah couldn't tolerate. The million reasons why this had been a bad idea smacked him in the gut, emptying out in a sigh of regret. It appeared that no good deed would go unpunished after all.

"Dad, you need to go get him. Victor didn't do anything wrong." Evan yanked his arm out of his grip and turned to leave the truck despite Isaiah's clear direction.

"Evan, we're going home. Victor and I will discuss this later."

"Dad!"

"Evan, you need to understand when a conversation is none of your business," he said, pulling out of the parking spot and heading for the exit. Evan slumped into the far side of his seat, body angled away from Isaiah and face a mask of impotent rage. Isaiah wasn't happy, either, and the fact that he'd just spoken so harshly to his son ratcheted it up even higher.

Isaiah cursed under his breath, planning everything he would discuss with his husband later.

Chapter Twelve

The body pressed against him was his for the taking.

The music pounded through the club, the strobe lights highlighting the writhing bodies dancing and groping and more on the floor. It was electric, the beats and the energy of the crowd; every song ramped up his adrenaline, taking him out of his body and out of the dilemma his life had become. He'd wanted an escape, and he'd found it.

Bodies swirled around him, and Victor let the legs and arms and hard groins brush against and grind into him as he lost his mind to the music. He'd deflected roaming hands and lingering looks all night, but the slighter of build, shorter Asian with a sexy smile and muscles to spare had his attention. He was as far from Isaiah as he could get in body type and build. Victor had considered finding a big guy with dark skin and chocolate brown eyes and fucking him until he didn't give a shit about his husband anymore or he just didn't give a shit in general. The idea had lost its appeal when every African-American man reminded him of the one he was trying to forget.

He'd left Isaiah and Evan in the truck, still stinging from the accusation that he would do anything that might harm his stepson, and went back into the rehearsal hall, fully intending to put in a few more hours of work and exhaust himself and his anger. But it hadn't worked, and he'd found himself in the showers, putting on clothes he left in the studio and taking an Uber to a gay dance club he'd gone to several times with Alan. It offered strong drinks, willing men, and anonymity.

Nobody cared who he was when he was here, and nobody cared about the gold band on his left hand.

And why should they when the man who'd put it there didn't care, either?

Victor grabbed his dance partner's hips and rubbed their bodies together again, leaning in close enough to feel the sharp exhale of the man's breath on his skin. The man was beautiful and eager, and Victor was tempted to bend him over a flat surface eventually, but for now he just wanted to lose himself in the oblivion of a heavy beat and a buzz.

As they swayed together the man leaned in and claimed Victor's mouth in a kiss, his mouth opening as he tried to deepen the kiss with his soft lips and warm tongue. Victor indulged for a few seconds with a groan that he felt down in his marrow. It was exhilarating to be wanted, a sexual balm to his wounded pride and sexual frustration. Jerking off wasn't cutting it. Yeah, it gave him release and a lingering lethargy that, for a short time, convinced him everything would be okay. That he wouldn't always want his husband. That it didn't sting when Isaiah pushed him away. That he didn't long for it to be different.

But it never lasted for long and he wondered if replacing his hand with a willing body would draw out the aftereffects. He'd never been a guy to sleep around. Victor wasn't a prude, and he would normally take what was on offer if he was with a consenting adult or two, and nobody was going to end up hurt.

The only one hurting tonight was him, and it would be the same tomorrow morning.

Victor's partner broke the kiss and reached for his hand, drawing him through the crowd toward the back room. His smile, flashed over his shoulder, was sexy, playful, and eager, and Victor's dick responded to the blatant invitation. He barely registered the couples and multiple pairings around them as they made their way to the back. Nobody noticed them, nobody cared except for the occasional sexy smile and silent inquiry of whether they wanted another to join the fun.

The space was a warren of partially hidden nooks and open spaces where groups could play and watch and be watched, but Victor was grateful when his partner led them to the corner, dark and hidden from too many eyes. The man shoved him against the wall, his touch now insistent and carnal, and so different from the exploratory touch of their lips on the dance floor. Victor was glad—he needed it, craved the passion and the fire he hadn't really experienced since that night with Isaiah.

Victor retreated from the thought of his husband and the dead end that clearly was coming. And what was he bitching about, anyway? He had the best of both worlds: a marriage of convenience that kept him safe and allowed him to pursue his activism and a hall pass to fuck anyone he wanted as long as he was discreet. It was any gay man's dream.

So why did it feel so wrong at the sight of his partner dropping to his knees on the floor in front of him, open hunger and carnal intent his only expression? Pushing aside his hesitation, Victor canted his hips forward, his own invitation hard to ignore. The guy didn't disappoint, agile fingers releasing his belt and the top button of his jeans, the metal of his zipper glinting in the low light as it was drawn down to expose him to his new friend.

Victor shut his eyes and leaned back against the wall to enjoy the ride. Isaiah's face popped up in his vision like the Ghost of Husbands Present, persistent and clamoring for attention. It was the same fantasy—made worse by the fact that it had happened—Isaiah's body blocking out the moonlight, mouth and hands making Victor writhe in pleasure.

Damn.

He snapped his eyes open, searching for something to erase the memory that made him crazy. Men were everywhere, moving against one another; none of them cared about the guy they couldn't have. But he did. And while he wasn't fooling himself about what he was to Isaiah, it wasn't his speed to use some other man to work through his shit. Maybe it was old-fashioned; he knew it was stupid, but it was what it was.

Victor gripped the hands of his companion, stopping him before he reached in to grip his dick, lifting him to his feet and cursing himself for the look of confusion and hurt on the man's face. Victor had dragged an innocent into his fucked-up life, and now he had to carry that with him. There was no explanation to give, that would make this better, so he leaned in and pressed a soft kiss to his mouth and gave him a smile that hopefully eased the sting a little bit.

Without a backward glance, he made his way to the exit and home.

He felt Isaiah behind him before he saw him.

Victor continued what he was doing, pouring orange juice into a glass and placing the pitcher back into the fridge. He shut the door and turned slowly, determined not to react until he could gauge the mood of his husband.

If Isaiah was spoiling for a fight, he'd get it.

If he wanted to talk about today like adults, he might get

that.

If he wanted to bend Victor over the island and take his ass? He could definitely have that.

If he wanted his heart? Well, he might already have it, but Victor was hoping he could reverse the trajectory of that missile, because he knew the only one in danger of getting blown apart in this situation was him.

Victor turned in time to see Isaiah enter the kitchen, shoulders bunched in hostility, and he squared off, leaning on the counter with contrived nonchalance. The two drinks he'd slammed back at the club had worn off a long time ago, and now he was nothing but raw nerves and brittle anger.

Isaiah stalked over, stopping within arm's length of him, and even in the dim light of the kitchen, he could feel his husband's gaze rake over his bare chest. Victor had been hot, sweat drying on his skin when he'd arrived home, and his shirt had been the first to go. He didn't try to cover up; let Isaiah deal with what he wanted but wouldn't let himself have.

"You took your time coming home," Isaiah said, his tone as flat as the granite countertop.

"I needed to blow off some steam," he replied, his accent heavy on his tongue tonight, a result of the drinks and his fatigue. He'd pay for it tomorrow on the rehearsal floor, but he didn't care. "The last place I wanted to be was here until I'd settled down."

"Two a.m.," Isaiah said, his gaze turning pointedly to the clock glowing on the surface of the microwave oven. "You've got rehearsal in the morning."

His anger had cooled, but Isaiah's words threw gasoline on the embers, and in a flash he was back to a three-alarm blaze.

"Well, he was worth it."

His first reaction to Isaiah's shocked expression was a mean and petty glee that his words had hit the mark. But as his husband's expression morphed into raw hurt, his victory was tarnished by shame of not only the lie, but also the smallness of the behavior. He wasn't that man, not a guy who hurt other people to make himself feel bigger.

"I see," Isaiah said, clearing his throat as he leaned heavily on the kitchen island, hands visibly unsteady, but his usual mask of calm and unconcern slamming down like a gate barring any access to the man underneath. "Well, I guess that's…" His jaw clenched like he was fighting back revealing any emotion, but his words gave him away. "You didn't waste any time."

"You told me you didn't want me and that I should look elsewhere. I did what you told me to do, Isaiah." He shrugged, hopefully transmitting a nonchalance he wasn't feeling at all.

The silence that stretched between them was even more pronounced in the stillness of the early morning. God, he wanted to tell him that nothing had happened with that guy because of him, to reopen this discussion and try to get another outcome, but Victor knew it was a waste of time. Isaiah had been nothing but clear. Victor was the one with the problem.

No time like the present to deal with another problem.

"About what happened today with Evan," he said, his words changing the subject so quickly that Isaiah paused, visibly taking a few seconds to get caught up.

"I can't have him exposed like that. Stephen and I built his life to be normal and away from all the bullshit of Hollywood and Los Angeles."

"My activism isn't bullshit, Isaiah," Victor said, interrupting him. "The reporters hit a nerve today when they called me a coward."

"You're not." Isaiah started to object, but Victor cut him off. This was his time to talk.

"I feel like one sometimes. I'm safe here, because of you, while my brothers and sisters are suffering, and that is why I can't stop talking about it. I have the freedom and the platform, and I'm using it because I can. I understand your concerns about your team, and I agree that Evan shouldn't be part of it, but I'm not going to stop." He took a breath and swallowed. "I figured it was a given considering how we ended up here."

Isaiah dipped his head, lifting to scrub at his two a.m. stubble. Victor let him think; nothing about this situation was easy. When he looked up again and their eyes locked across the darkened kitchen, Victor knew how hard this was on Isaiah. His dark eyes were roiling with emotions, and none of them were good, except for the flashes of desire. That was good, except for the fact that it would never lead anywhere.

"I know how we got here, but I can't let our arrangement derail my life, Evan's life."

He didn't say it out loud, but the word "temporary" hung in the air. Victor wasn't expected to be around forever, and that hurt. It was as simple as that. And it made his next suggestion very easy to say.

"My place here in the L.A. company isn't guaranteed." Isaiah's expression was confused, but understanding took over as he continued his solution. "Other companies are interested. London, Paris, and New York have all been vocal about wanting me to come there. I'll be going to New York in a few weeks to do a special performance, and I think they'll offer me a spot as a principal dancer. If I take it, then it could solve our problems. Not even the immigration people could dispute a legitimate job offer."

"I didn't mean you had to leave," Isaiah said, his tone full of the regret that also tightened his jaw. "I don't *want* you to have to leave."

Before the events of the last couple of days, Victor would have indulged in his hopeless romanticism, but this time he wouldn't make that mistake. Isaiah had been clear, honest, and Victor would be the same. It was the least they owed each other.

He opened the dishwasher and placed his glass inside. Victor passed his husband, suddenly wanting nothing more than his own bed. "I know you aren't telling me to go, Isaiah, but you aren't exactly asking me to stay, either."

Chapter Thirteen

"Isaiah, your husband is hot."

He turned from the bar to face the man with the smirk, his dimples obscured by the scruffy beard on his face. His overly long hair was in stark contrast to the designer tuxedo he wore, but Matt made it work. He always made it work in every area of his life.

"Damn, what is that on your face, Matt?"

His friend rubbed his palm across his face, subtly flipping Isaiah the bird at the same time. They both laughed, and Isaiah placed his drink on the bar and pulled Matt Ames into a fierce hug. College roommates, both on athletic scholarships, they'd been best friends and sometimes lovers as they navigated the world of competitive sports and being gay in that world. A gold medal decathlete, now Matt owned Fierce, a pro-level fitness apparel and equipment company, and Isaiah couldn't be prouder of him.

"The beard is awesome," Matt answered, motioning to the bartender to give him what Isaiah was having. He looked good in his black tie, happy. "You're so dazzled by the new hotness in your life that you can't see mine anymore. I get it. I'm okay with it."

"You're an idiot."

"Tell me something new," Matt said, taking his drink from the bartender with a grin and a tip. "But the thing you have to tell me is that you're going to sign on as one of my first celebrity endorsements. I know Ian told you about the offer."

"He did, and I'm in." Isaiah followed his friend through the crowd of overdressed athletes, spouses, agents, owners, and journalists. This annual awards dinner for sports journalism was always a well-attended gathering, and he'd been tapped to present an award. Now that all the formalities were over, everyone was winding down, and the party was cranking up. "You know I believe in your company and your vision, and I'll do whatever I can to help you out."

"Thanks, man. I've hired the Barclay Group to plan the coordinated publicity, photo shoots, and appearances. I'll have pro and amateur endorsements and have key events to support LGBTQ athletes with awareness, camps for youth, and scholarships."

"You never do anything halfway, Matt, and you always make it happen."

"I learned from the best, Isaiah. I've told you a million times how you pushed me to be better, train harder, work longer."

"We did that for each other, I think. Stephen always said that we didn't need crowds yelling our name as long as we had each other." He smiled at the memories he had with this man, brother and friend, godfather to Evan. "I think we've achieved everything we wrote on that whiteboard in our room."

"I think we did." Matt smiled at him, glancing around the room and nodding toward a huge Latino man with a shaved head holding up one of the pillars in the room. Javier Rojas, former MMA Heavyweight Champion, was surrounded by his usual entourage of trainers, managers, and women with fake breasts. "I'm going to use your name to reel in that huge fish. So far he's been blowing me off, but I want him." Matt smirked when Isaiah chuckled at his choice of words. Javier was Matt's type, so his innuendo wasn't off base. "I want him on my endorsement roster."

"And in your bed." Isaiah said what they were both thinking, dodging Matt's punch to his arm and barely avoiding spilling his drink. He knew his friend very well, and Rojas checked all of Matt's boxes.

"He's disappointingly straight. I've checked."

"I bet you did."

"Sorry I couldn't make the party to celebrate you finding the last hot gay man in Los Angeles," Matt said, changing the subject to the one that Isaiah knew he wouldn't be able to avoid. "It happened so fast, and I couldn't get back from Callanos."

"It was fast." Isaiah shifted in the middle of the crowd, looking around to see who was listening. He was in a room of reporters, after all. "Victor was…sudden."

He searched the room for his husband, who'd peeled away from him as soon as the awards portion of the evening was over. To describe their relationship since their talk a week ago as chilly wouldn't be accurate; there was too much of the fire of anger and resentment underneath it all. Victor was putting distance between them because he was hurt. Isaiah let it happen because he was sorry, and proximity would only lead him to temptation, and temptation was a direct path to Victor's bed.

Isaiah found him, his tall frame draped in a collarless, black tuxedo with non-traditional skinny pants that showed off his muscular ass and thighs to perfection. He wore no tie, a single dark stud fastening the collar of his white shirt. His only other jewelry was a platinum stud in his left ear and his wedding band. When he'd descended the steps of the house, Isaiah had grabbed the railing of the staircase to catch his breath.

His husband caught almost everyone's eye in the room, male and female. Victor was sex-on-a-stick. Isaiah resented the way that people ogled him, but the prickle of jealousy when Victor looked back was like a hot knife in his gut. But it was the flash of sexual interest in his husband's eyes when he was talking to a pro soccer player that had led to his second whiskey. He'd obsessively speculated about who Victor had been with that night, reliving the sight of him half naked in the kitchen smelling of sweat and another man.

All Isaiah had wanted to do was strip him down and erase the trace of anyone else. Instead, he'd driven him away. It had killed him but it was probably for the best. But there were just as many people who weren't enthralled by his husband. Masiello had visibly blanched when he'd gotten a good look at Victor tonight. And several of his teammates, not his friends on the team, had exchanged shitty smiles and raised eyebrows. Assholes.

"I was surprised when I heard the news. He's not your usual type, Isaiah." Matt leaned in closer, also mindful that this was a room full of professional eavesdroppers. "He's wearing makeup."

Charcoal and silver eyeliner rimmed his blue eyes and made him look like a fairy creature, an elf maybe. But it was his mouth that was sinful, his full lips accented with a subtle gloss. The effect made Isaiah want to lean in and lick at them until Victor opened to his invasion. Victor must have felt his eyes on him, because he turned his face, eyes locking in right away. Holy shit. Would he ever look at that man and not want him?

Isaiah tried to cover up his groan by taking a sip of his drink, breaking the connection with his husband. He turned back to Matt, who was watching him with a bemused expression on his face.

"I see." Matt full-on grinned now, like he had just been given the secret chicken recipe by the Colonel himself.

"You don't see anything." Isaiah rushed to correct his friend of his clearly wrong idea about his marriage. He leaned over, making sure only Matt could hear. "It was an arrangement to keep him from getting deported."

Matt pulled back, his eyebrows raised in surprise. "So, the ugly rumor is true."

Isaiah didn't bother to ask what rumor. He'd figured that's what people would say.

"It was the right thing to do." And then he considered the other part of the equation. "He might not be here for much longer. His post in L.A. is up soon, and he's not guaranteed to get a permanent spot."

"And how do you feel about that?"

"Evan will miss him. They've bonded."

"Way to avoid the conversation."

"There's nothing more to say," Isaiah answered stubbornly

"So, you don't mind that Eric Tolle is practically groping his ass right now?"

Isaiah swung around so fast his drink spilled over his hand, dripping on his fingers and down the front of his dress pants. He swore under his breath, shaking off the moisture, as he took in the scene before him.

Eric Tolle. Hand resting right above, if not actually *on*, Victor's ass.

The only thing that kept his rage in check was the way his husband tried to put distance between them. He didn't push him away altogether, though, and Isaiah couldn't help but remember that Victor had taken at least a temporary lover two nights before. Eric was always up for anything, and anybody, and everyone knew it.

The fact that Victor was allowing his touch in front of all these people at an event that was work related for Isaiah stung, but it was the personal aspect that made him a little nuts. His jealousy, as ridiculous and selfish as it was, propelled him across the room to his husband.

Did he mind that Eric Tolle was groping Victor?

Fuck yeah, he did.

Chapter Fourteen

The man could not take a hint.

Victor had continued the conversation only because this man, Eric something, had told him he wanted to interview him about his activism and the upcoming charity event in NYC to benefit AIDS education. The reporter had said that he wanted to do an in-depth article, but it was clear from the way his hand kept drifting all over Victor's body that the only thing he wanted to get deep into was his ass.

It was never going to happen. He wasn't even close to Victor's type.

His type was walking toward him with a face full of thunder and eyes blazing.

"Eric," Isaiah said when he stopped in front of the two of them. He spoke to the reporter, but he stared at Victor while reaching his arm around his waist to remove Eric's hand from the small of his back. The possessiveness thrilled Victor, but the audacity to try to claim what he'd clearly told Victor he didn't want, pissed him off.

"Isaiah, I was just setting up an interview time with

Victor," Eric said, moving closer to the two of them, his hand holding out a business card where it was poised between the small amount of space between their bodies.

"That's business," Isaiah said, his eyes dark and glittering with heat. "This is a party."

Victor watched as his husband reached up and plucked the card out of Eric's hand, inserting it in the inside pocket of Victor's jacket. His skin was warm through the silken fabric of his dress shirt, and the touch made Victor suck in a breath, letting it out on a slow exhale as he tried to get his breathing and his hardening cock under control. He found the strength to turn to look at Eric, forcing a smile past the growl he wanted to levy at his husband.

"Eric, I'll be in touch about the interview. Thank you so much." He made the move to reach out and shake his hand, but Isaiah tugged him closer, effectively barring him from being polite. He waited until the man had left with an arched brow and barely disguised expression of disgust before he turned his anger on his husband. "What the fuck was that?"

Isaiah wrapped his arm around him tighter, bringing their bodies in full contact. To anyone else in the room they probably looked like a happy newlywed couple who could barely keep their hands off each other. What a joke.

"That was me making sure you didn't show me up in front of all my colleagues with the sluttiest man in town."

"I had it handled."

"With his hand all over your ass?" Isaiah scoffed, his laugh brittle and dark. "You didn't have anything handled."

"Isaiah, it's so good to see you."

His husband froze, fingers digging into his waist at the sound of the man's voice. As Victor watched, Isaiah closed his eyes for the briefest second and, when he opened them again, he stared at Victor with a message he didn't understand.

"Mr. Masiello." Isaiah smiled as he turned to the man now

standing at their side. "It's nice to see you. Can I introduce my husband, Victor Aleksandrov?"

Victor turned and took in the man standing next to him. He was shorter than either of them, stocky and olive-skinned, his outward appearance a testament to his Italian last name. He was smiling at the two of them, but his eyes traveled up and down Victor's body. He was sure Mr. Masiello was convinced he had the perfect poker face, but he gave away everything he was thinking.

And what he was thinking was that Isaiah's husband was a little bit too gay for his liking.

Victor shook off Isaiah's grip, held out his hand to his husband's boss, and smiled as friendly as he could make it with his anger just below the surface.

"It's nice to meet you, Mr. Masiello."

The man took his hand in a firm grip that he quickly released and gestured to other men standing nearby. They were all big men, as wide as a standard doorframe, and all wearing expressions of interest or disdain with their formal wear.

Isaiah took over the introductions, reciting the names of his teammates, but Victor knew he'd never remember them all. He was too busy battling the unease now creeping up his spine and mixing with his own anger. Masiello speaking to him pulled his attention back to the man who would make or break Isaiah's career.

"Will you be at the games this season, Victor?" His smile turned self-conscious and apologetic. "Of course, being a ballerina you probably have no interest in sports."

He had no words and no answer to the question. He and Isaiah had never spoken about his attending games. Hell, he might not even be here when the new season began in a few months. He glanced at Isaiah and hoped that he read his subtle nod correctly.

"Of course. I'll have to consider my own performance schedule, but I'll be there as much as I can."

"We'll save you a seat with the cheerleaders."

All of them, Victor, Isaiah, and Masiello, swiveled their heads toward the players, but it was impossible to know which one had said it. Masiello turned scarlet, and Isaiah moved to confront his teammates.

"What did you say?" Isaiah asked, his voice low, but as brittle as glass. Only a few people around them turned to watch what was going on, but his husband didn't give them a show. He was so used to living his life on the down low that he didn't even cause a scene when he was ready to throw down.

Masiello stepped between them, his hands outstretched as if he had the strength to stop any of them if they decided to let this escalate to actual violence. The other players backed down one by one, retreating with flat expressions, none of them apologetic or embarrassed.

The boss man turned back to the two of them, his own expression a "what can you do" chagrin.

"That was unfortunate," Masiello said, adding a shrug to his words. "This is all going to take some getting used to for the team, the fans. We're not used to having a…a husband… among the ranks."

And just like that, Victor was done.

"It was nice meeting you, but I've got an early rehearsal tomorrow morning," Victor said, turning to his husband with a smile that made his own face ache with the effort to make it. "I can send the car back for you if you need to stay longer."

He didn't wait for an answer.

Their car was nice.

It was a big, black glossy BMW with blackened windows

and a privacy screen inside. Their driver had met them at the curb once they'd called, and he'd pulled away into the night, the lights of Los Angeles flying past them as they sat inside, surrounded by a silence heavy with anger and frustration.

Victor cursed in his native tongue, calling Isaiah and Masiello and Eric and those asshole football players every nasty word he could think of.

"I can't understand a goddamn word you're saying," Isaiah said from his side of the back seat. "If you want to say something, then just fucking say it."

Victor didn't even know where to start, so he picked the lowest hanging fruit. "Your friends are fucking homophobes."

"They aren't my friends. They're my teammates." Victor scoffed at that, and Isaiah pinned him with a glare that kept his cock hard. It was kind of sick how a fierce Isaiah flipped his switch. "I'm sure you have dicks in the ballet. You work together, but you're not friends."

Victor couldn't argue with that, but it did nothing to ease the anger roiling in his gut. Bottom line: he was spoiling for a fight, and he was going to get one.

He shifted closer to his husband on the seat, leaning in to force eye contact. "So, will I be the first gay man to attend the games or something? Didn't Stephen attend? What was the ballerina thing?"

Isaiah dipped his head, his hand rubbing against his face before he answered. "Stephen went to my games."

"Huh. So, what did he mean by that?" He examined his husband's face, waiting to see if he'd answer him. Victor knew what it was, he just didn't know if Isaiah would admit it. When his husband broke eye contact, he got tired of waiting. "I'm never going to pass for straight, Isaiah. Even without the makeup, I'm gay."

"Yeah, everybody figured that out when you were eye fucking Eric Tolle."

Oh, that was too much. Isaiah didn't want him, but nobody else could have him? Fuck that.

"Really? Did that make you jealous?"

Isaiah's gaze snapped back to his own, his pupils blown and eyes dark with his anger or arousal. Probably both. The lights of the city cast his profile in intermittent shadow, and the result was hide-and-seek of his beautiful face. Victor moved in closer, resting his hand on Isaiah's thigh, close enough to his groin to feel the weight of his cock against the side of his hand. His fingers itched to reach out and stroke him, but he waited, wondering what Isaiah would do.

When he didn't push him away, Victor shifted his hand higher, palming Isaiah's hard dick through the fabric of his dress pants. With the mixture of adrenaline and anger racing side by side through his system, Victor just wanted to fuck or fight. Isaiah's choice.

"Does it make you hard to think of me with someone else?" Victor asked, scanning his face and filing every reaction on his face, the smell of his skin and aftershave, the pounding of his pulse in his neck.

He leaned in all the way, unable to resist the pull of the soft spot of flesh below his ear, nibbling and sucking on it, and then traveling upward to pull on the sweet curve of his lobe. Isaiah shuddered beneath him, pulling away only slightly as if to avoid the intensity of his reaction and not the pleasure. Victor chased the retreat of his body, licking and biting at the firm column of his neck, loving the vibration of his groan underneath his mouth.

"Victor, baby," Isaiah said and moved to push against his chest but digging his fingers into his shoulders instead. "The driver…"

"Can get his own dick to suck," Victor said, gripping his husband's strong jaw and tugging him close for a kiss. Isaiah wanted it, his mouth opening the minute their lips touched, and Victor slid his tongue inside his wet heat. He tasted so good, like whisky and Isaiah, sin and redemption. He surrendered, melting against Victor with a moan that spoke of the nights they'd spent apart. The sounds turned him on, made him ache for more...everything.

"Come here," Victor said, tugging Isaiah up off the seat and over his body until he straddled Victor's lap. "I fucking missed you."

Isaiah went wild on top of him, grinding his groin against Victor's abdomen, seeking the friction he craved. His fingers plucked at Victor's shirt, tugging at the stud and then clutching at the seat cushion behind him when their bodies aligned perfectly and hard dick slid against hard dick.

"I missed you, too...damn." He didn't complete the sentence, unable to finish the sentence. It was beyond hot to see the usually controlled man lose control. It was incredible to watch him try to get off by writhing against his body.

Victor reached between them and quickly unfastened Isaiah's belt, button, and zipper even with hands shaking with his own need. He slipped his hand inside Isaiah's pants and briefs, shoving them down his thighs and exposing his cock to his hungry gaze. Thick and dark and wet at the head, it pointed toward him, begging for his touch. Victor wrapped his hand around it, slowly and deliberately stroking the shaft, coaxing him to fuck into his grip.

When Isaiah's hips bucked forward, Victor leaned up and bit at his lower lip with a growl. "You watched me, now it's my turn to watch you."

Victor kept his eyes on Isaiah, watching the comprehension flicker over his face when he let go of his cock and waited until Isaiah took over, wrapping his long fingers around the rigid flesh and pumping slowly. Victor didn't know what was better, the sight of his own pale flesh against his husband's darker tone or the vision of Isaiah fucking his own fist in a scene from the world's hottest porno.

Isaiah moaned, and Victor lifted his eyes to his face, sucking a breath at the heart-stoppingly aroused expression on his face. Victor tapped his fingers against Isaiah's lips. "Suck on them. I want them wet."

Isaiah opened his mouth, eyes focused on Victor's as he sucked his fingers inside and coated them with saliva, tongue flicking up and down and between the digits. When he withdrew them, they were wet and glistening.

"Sit up and push your ass out," he ordered, and Isaiah obeyed, rising up and leaning forward, his back hitting the interior roof of the car with a light thud. Victor skimmed the sweet, taut globes of his ass, reached around, and pressed a finger inside him. He was tight, hot, and opened to his invasion so sweetly.

Isaiah pushed back on his hand, drawing him in deeper as he bit his bottom lip and pumped his dick at faster pace. Victor eased in deeper, pressing on his prostate and eating up the vision before him. His husband was gorgeous, debauched, and out of control, and he couldn't rip his eyes away for a second. Victor added another finger to Isaiah's hole, his own erection pressing painfully against the confines of his pants at the shudder that ran through his lover's body.

"Good, yes?" His accent was heavy on his tongue, and he babbled in a mixture of his native language and English, telling Isaiah how beautiful he was, how much he wanted to fuck him, how his surrender made his heart clench tightly in his chest, things he could never say out loud. Things that were not wanted. "Yeah, just like that."

Isaiah was riding his fingers now, rising and falling in the same rhythm he stroked himself with slick, firm strokes.

"I'd love to bend you over and taste your ass. Stick my tongue into you, fuck you with my mouth." Isaiah whimpered, his pace faltering at the words. "You'd like that, wouldn't you?

You like the makeup." He leaned up and bit on his earlobe, murmuring low with dark carnality. "You wouldn't care if I fucked you wearing panties or lingerie? I get you hot, don't I, Isaiah?"

His husband groaned above him, his voice raw and ragged and broken as his body stiffened and he shot come all over Victor's shirt and jacket. Victor pressed his fingers deeper inside Isaiah's body, watching avidly as the shudders and aftershocks rolled through his big, muscled body. When Isaiah opened his eyes, hazy with pleasure, they focused on his.

Victor eased his fingers out of his lover, leaning upward to press a brief kiss to his lips as the car came to a stop in front of their house. Victor saw the flicker of hesitation on his husband's face, and he knew he had to keep him here, not allow him to retreat again.

"Fasten your pants and get inside." He kissed him again, making sure he had his full attention. "Then take them off, because I'm going to fuck you."

Chapter Fifteen

This was insanity, and he was eager to lose his mind.

Isaiah's fingers fumbled with the keys for a second or two, but he got the door open and reached back to grab Victor's arm and drag him into the house. He had enough sense not to linger in the foyer, mindful of Evan and his mother, Esther, asleep upstairs. Victor understood, following as silently as he could. They stumbled on the stairs, hands and fingers fumbling with buttons and studs and zippers.

They reached the upstairs landing, and Victor hauled him close for a kiss. It was sloppy and wet and hot, and Isaiah bit back a groan when his spent dick tingled with the anticipation of being touched by this man again. He laughed; he was a grown man, a father, and his body was reacting like a horny teenager. Just give him a few minutes, and he'd be ready to go.

Isaiah pulled out of the kiss, tugging his husband toward their end of the floor where they could rid themselves of all these clothes and take full advantage of a bed. When they reached the door to his room, the one he'd shared with Stephen, he hesitated. He thought it was only a moment, but it was long enough for Victor to notice and remove his touch from Isaiah's body.

Their gazes locked, and he saw the hurt and anger in the set of Victor's jaw and the compression of his full, sensual lips into a thin line. Isaiah wasn't ready to invite this man into his bed, Stephen's bed, their bed, no matter how much he wanted him, and he felt like it had become a deal breaker. The last wedge between them. Victor nodded in understanding and moved forward, stopping in front of his door and opening it. When he stepped inside, Victor left it open.

It was up to Isaiah.

He wanted Victor, and clearly trying to keep away from him wasn't working All it did was lead to anger and jealousy. He closed the distance as quickly as he could, on legs shaking with desire and want, shutting the door behind him and turning the lock.

Victor stood next to his bed, jacket off, working on removing the studs from his shirt. He looked up from his task, and Isaiah sucked in a breath at the sight of him. He was beautiful, passion and desire reddening his cheeks, and his lips were swollen from their kisses in the car. He stalked toward Isaiah, shoved him against the door, pressing their bodies together from chest to thigh.

"What can I have?" Victor asked, the words poignant on many levels. There were so many boundaries and rules between them, but some would fall tonight.

"Anything," Isaiah answered, bucking his hips forward to emphasize his point. "My ass. My mouth. Anything you want."

Victor growled, muttering in Russian before sliding his hands over Isaiah's chest and pushing his jacket off his shoulders. "Get naked. I'll get the stuff."

Isaiah watched him cross the room to the nightstand, retrieve a condom and bottle of lube, and toss them on the bed. He returned to his side and mumbled something about him not moving fast enough as he attacked Isaiah's clothes. They made quick work of the barriers between them, ignoring the sounds of fabric tearing and buttons popping to finally get the contact they both craved. Isaiah was shivery, needy, wanting nothing but the feel of Victor's body on top of his to keep him from breaking. It was not a feeling he liked, but he leaned in to it, knowing it would make getting fucked all the better.

Victor read his mind and shoved him down onto the bed and lay on top of him. They were so similar in height that chests, cocks, and tangled legs aligned perfectly. Isaiah writhed underneath him, unable to touch enough of him, to feel enough of him. They kissed, languid and deep, exploring each other's mouths. Victor tasted of the drinks at the party and his own brand of wicked temptation.

Isaiah held him tight, nuzzling his nose along Victor's jawline and down his neck, licking and tasting his skin and sweat as Victor shifted, reached, and grabbed the lube. The sound of the cap popping off made goose bumps spread over Isaiah's skin, his dick hard and leaking as it rubbed between their bodies. He mourned the loss of contact when Victor eased back onto his knees, shifting Isaiah's body to expose his hole to his gaze, his touch.

Slick fingers, cold with the lubricant, pressed at his entrance. First around the tight ring of flesh, massaging and coaxing until he opened to his penetration. One long digit, then two, then three stretched him as Victor kissed, bit, and sucked every part of Isaiah he could reach.

"You're so beautiful, baby," Victor crooned, his voice husky with desire and thick with his accent.

English interspersed with Russian, words he didn't need to translate to understand what they meant. Isaiah was wanted, desired, needed. He licked his dry lips, intending to confess the same, to admit that Victor was someone he couldn't resist, that there was something about him that awakened parts of Isaiah he thought he'd buried along with Stephen. But then his husband pressed inside and grazed his prostrate, and all Isaiah could do was grab his cock and stroke it with a palm slick with his own pre-come.

"You look so good, baby," Victor urged above him as he opened the condom, slid it down his length, and then slathered it with lube. Isaiah watched his progress, arching upward when Victor stroked his lube-slick palm over his own erection, forcing out a groan that broke through on a gasp. "Open up, let me in."

Isaiah lifted his knees in invitation, gasping at the nudge of the head of Victor's cock against his opening. He breathed out, willing his body to relax as his husband pushed inside, inch by inch, ragged moan by ragged moan. The burn was painful at first, but he leaned into it, knowing that the pleasure would be even more exquisite.

Isaiah wrapped his legs around Victor's waist, surprised at how much he wanted to submit to this man, craved it. With Stephen, it had been an easy give and take, but the men since him hadn't included anyone he trusted or wanted to fuck him. But with Victor inside him, moving and filling and stretching and taking him, it was different, something he would beg for, something he would begin to need.

Panic rose in his chest at the direction of his thoughts. This was what he'd been afraid of, terrified that Victor was different and that he'd put something more at risk than just a physical vulnerability.

"Hey, stay with me," his lover urged, his hips moving in a slow rhythm, his mouth gliding along his cheek before pressing down a kiss guaranteed to rein his focus back in. "What do you need?"

"I need you to fuck me. Hard," Isaiah said, hoping his husband understood his need, the need to get out of his head and away from the space where fear of hurt controlled his decisions. He needed him to fuck him until he couldn't think about anything but Victor and his cock and coming.

Victor understood perfectly.

"Fuck," Victor moaned as he pulled out of his body, only to drive back in, harder, faster, the lube slicking the way but doing nothing to relieve the almost unbearable pressure. He leaned back on his knees, his hips slapping against Isaiah's ass as his fingers dug into his flesh. There would be bruises later, and Isaiah shivered at the idea of wearing his marks, Victor's desire imprinted on his skin.

"You should…" Victor licked his lips, soothing the marks from where he'd been biting. "You should see how pretty your hole stretches around my cock. You're so dark, and I'm so pale. It's fucking beautiful."

Isaiah squeezed his eyes shut, the tightening of his balls the first sign that he was close. Victor shifted against him, raising one of Isaiah's legs to rest on his shoulder, and the angle caused the head of his dick to slide against his prostate on every withdrawal and relentless reentry.

Isaiah cried out in pleasure, and Victor took it as a sign to continue the pounding that shoved them higher and higher across the bed. Isaiah lifted his arms to place his palms against the headboard, and the added resistance made the aftershocks of the thrusts just that much sweeter. Pain and pleasure mixed in the roughness of the sex, Victor's tender touches and grazing of his lips against whatever part of Isaiah's skin he could reach pushing everything to the realm of almost overwhelming.

He opened his eyes, soaking in the sight of his husband so focused on him, sweat slicking back his long, dark hair, blue eyes almost black with arousal. It was too much, waking up primal things inside of him he knew he should keep to himself.

Like how he didn't want anyone else to ever see Victor like this or feel his cock filling them up with his thick, hard length. He didn't want his mouth kissing anyone else or saying the nasty, carnal things he was uttering with each deep thrust.

Isaiah palmed his own dick, reaching for the orgasm tingling at the edge of his senses, knowing it was the one thing that would stop his mind from going to places it had no business venturing. One second he had himself in hand and the next he was pushed aside and Victor's long, pale fingers were wrapped around him, stroking in time with his thrusts.

His body gave no real warning before he was arching off the bed, back bowed as his channel clenched around Victor's erection. It was intense and real, and he wallowed in the moment with this man, allowing pleasure to wash over his skin without any worries about what was going to happen tomorrow or even five minutes from now.

Victor shouted something above him, half Russian and half English, as his body stiffened with his own orgasm. Isaiah stared, mesmerized, while the taut muscles and strong body arched in ecstasy. It was beautiful, reminiscent of the way his husband surrendered to the music and the dance when he was onstage. No wonder crowds clamored to see him perform. Isaiah would never be able to watch him without remembering this moment.

Victor fell across his body, elbows catching the brunt of his weight and cushioning the impact of hard body hitting hard body. They were slick with sweat and Isaiah's come between them, but neither of them cared as their mouths met in a kiss that was more sweet nothings than carnal promise. Victor sighed and slid off him, thudding onto the bed beside him in a boneless heap of long limbs, heaving breaths, and deep sighs.

Victor took off the condom, tied it, and tossed it in the trash can before settling back beside Isaiah on the bed. They stared at each other across the pillow, and suddenly all the things Isaiah had been holding back and avoiding with him seemed off, wrong. Well, they just didn't seem right.

"That was…"

"Yes, it was," Victor answered with a grin and a silly waggle of his eyebrows.

Isaiah huffed out a laugh, watching his husband closely, remembering the night they'd first gotten together and everything was easy. The events of the evening, of the last couple of weeks, hit him hard, and suddenly he needed to clear the air.

"Victor, I'm sorry."

He shook his head, breaking eye contact to twist the tangled sheets in his fingers. "There's nothing for you to be sorry for."

"There's lots for me to be sorry for."

Victor leaned up on an elbow, dark hair falling into his eyes when he cocked his head at him. Isaiah reached up and pushed the strand out of his eyes, leaning in to press a soft kiss on his mouth. His husband shifted, climbing half on top of him, deepening the kiss for a moment before pulling back to stare down at Isaiah.

Isaiah searched for the right words to fill this moment. To apologize for all the shit that had been going down between them for weeks. Tonight had just been the culmination of all the stupid rules and boundaries he'd set up to keep Victor at arm's length.

"I'm going to say some stuff, and you're going to shut up and listen." Victor interrupted his thoughts, the quirk of his lip almost a smile, and it did a little to soften the seriousness of his tone. Isaiah slid a hand up Victor's side with the idea that he could anchor him in place and eliminate the distance he could feel developing between them. "What you did for me was…amazing."

"No," Isaiah said. He didn't want gratitude from Victor.

"I'm talking. Shut up," Victor said. "You probably saved my life, so I'm going to thank you." He eyeballed Isaiah, making sure he was going to keep quiet. "But I'm going to take the job in New York if they offer it to me."

"What? Why?"

"After tonight, I think it's for the best. The job will give us the perfect cover to be apart for the government, and it will just be better. I don't want to cause problems with your team, and I'm not going to stop speaking out." He chuckled, rolling off Isaiah to flop onto his back, turning his head to look at him with a grin that looked nothing like the one he'd started looking forward to seeing. "I can't promise that I won't march in drag in a Pride parade, but at least it won't be on your front doorstep."

Isaiah felt like shit, his chest heavy with his regret and disappointment in himself. Disappointment in a world that couldn't see how great Victor was. "Victor, no. Tonight was a mess, and my teammates…they'll get used to you."

"Maybe, but you're not going to have to worry about that. Evan won't be in the middle of anything that will disrupt the life you've made for him."

Victor reached over and placed his palm on his cheek, his thumb stroking across the skin in a slow motion that Isaiah leaned into and closed his eyes. He was saying everything Isaiah had wanted to hear, but somehow he didn't want it. Not really. But how did he ask him to stay when he still wasn't sure what he could offer in the long run?

Because good sex, amazing sex, didn't wipe out the reason it had been smart to not get emotionally involved with Victor Aleksandrov.

His husband rolled back over, so close now that Isaiah could feel his breath on his lips, the playful brush of their mouths. Isaiah leaned into it, but Victor pulled back.

"This is for the best. For you and Evan."

"What about you?" he asked, watching as Victor slid off the bed and padded toward the bathroom.

His lover stopped in the doorway, framed in the backlight of the night-light in the bathroom, his smile bright but missing his eyes completely. Even lying, he was beautiful. "Me? I'm fine."

Chapter Sixteen

"Esther, please show me how to make fried chicken."

Isaiah watched as Victor leaned over to his mother and gave her a kiss on the cheek, sneaking another piece of chicken off the plate next to her on the table. She swatted at him, shoving him away with a furious blush on her cheeks and a grin that made her dimples pop. She was smitten with his husband and wouldn't be the only one who would miss him when he went to New York.

Evan had taken the news hard when Victor had told him about the job. They'd explained that it might not happen but tried to prepare him for the real future where Victor would have to live somewhere else for work. While the Los Angeles job wasn't off the table, they'd come to an unspoken understanding that he wouldn't pursue it.

It was an understanding that Isaiah reconsidered about every other minute.

"Mama, do not show him how to make that chicken. I'll never get the flour cleaned up," Isaiah said teasingly, dodging his husband's elbow to his side.

"Yeah, Grandma. Victor's a good cook, but he makes the biggest mess." Evan joined in, ducking when Victor reached into his glass and tossed an ice cube at his head. They both laughed, sticking their tongues out at each other, and Isaiah smiled, wondering just how quiet it was going to seem around the house without Victor and his constant loop of Kylie Minogue and obsession with single shooter video games.

Too quiet.

"Don't feed them when I'm gone, Esther." Victor glared at them. "Let them starve for their lies and horrible accusations."

"I don't want you to go," Esther said, giving Isaiah the stink eye across the table. "None of us do, just in case we didn't say it."

Victor paused, dipping his head in acknowledgment before squeezing Esther's hand. "Thank you."

"I'm going to New York with you. I need to go shopping and spend some of Isaiah's money," his mother said, winking traitorously.

"You can come live with me, and we'll scandalize everyone with our love. I'll be your boy toy." Victor leaned in to give her another kiss, but she shoved him away, scooting back from the table to grab the pitcher of lemonade off the counter of the outdoor kitchen. It was a gorgeous day, but hot, and she walked around the table offering to top off everyone's beverage.

Mick and Piper were here, his cousin's arm wrapped around his wife's shoulders as they traded kisses and bites of food. They were always fun to watch, the unlikely pair who made it work. It wasn't perfect; he'd seen them fight, but they made it work.

Isaiah looked over at Victor, his chest tight with a pressure that had been there since last night in bed. Not even waking up with him, kissing and rubbing together until they'd both come, had relieved the weight of Victor's words. And now, him making his mama laugh and inspiring hero-worship in Evan…didn't make it any easier to breathe.

"You know," Mick drawled, his grin letting Isaiah know that he'd busted him staring at his husband and probably knew just what he'd been thinking. "I know your wedding wasn't exactly the most run-of-the-mill, but you never did partake of that other, super-fun wedding tradition."

"The what?" Isaiah took a sip of his drink, already suspicious of Mick's shit-eating grin. "What are you talking about?"

"The honeymoon."

"The what?" he said stupidly, the hot curl of awareness in his belly.

"You know the time when newly married people hide away to—" Mick stuttered when Piper nudged him and nodded toward Evan. "…play checkers."

Isaiah stared at Mick for a moment and then shook his head, chuckling. "What do you suggest?"

"I've got my estate in Hawaii." Mick grinned at Piper and she blushed at whatever shared memory passed between them. "You guys can use it."

She ignored his stare and added her own two cents. "We love Lake Como and the Caribbean."

"I know you've traveled with the ballet, Victor. Have you ever been to those places?" Mick asked.

Victor shook his head. "No. I've been so busy working. I keep meaning to finally take a vacation to the beach, but it has been so busy." He shrugged. "It's on my list."

"I can watch Evan for you," Isaiah's mama added, jumping with excitement at the turn of the discussion. "You two should get away before Victor has to go to work in New York or wherever."

Isaiah looked at his husband in disbelief. Were they the only two people who remembered that this marriage wasn't real? Victor's smile was lopsided, tentative, but he could see that his husband would have loved to have gone to any of those places. Isaiah hated that he had done anything to dampen his enthusiasm for life, that this marriage had made Victor hesitant to speak up and say what he clearly wanted.

"Sadly, we don't have time," Victor said, rising to his feet and gathering the dirty plates. "I have my last performances here in L.A., and I'm rehearsing for the benefit in New York."

He smiled at all of them and moved toward the house, and Isaiah couldn't take his eyes off of him. He moved with grace, his body strong and sexy, and everything from the ripple of his muscles to the sway of his tight ass under the fabric of his shorts turned him on. He couldn't stop thinking about last night; every touch of Victor's hand still played across his skin in a heated memory.

Victor had effectively put them in a box last night, and he'd done it for Isaiah. For Evan.

Isaiah could do something for him.

"I'll take those plates," Isaiah said as he rose from his seat and gathered more of the empty dishes to take with him when he sought out Victor. He found him in the kitchen, busily rinsing plates and placing them in the dishwasher. His shoulders and back muscles tensed, and Isaiah sensed that Victor knew exactly who it was who had joined him. Victor glanced over his shoulder, his smile warm and genuine, and the kindness of it in the midst of all their internal drama and uncertainty made Isaiah more determined than ever.

Isaiah placed his handful of dishes in the sink and then sidled up behind Victor, looping his arms around his waist, resting his chin on his shoulder until Victor relaxed against him on a sigh. He lifted his hands and tangled his fingers with Isaiah's, saying nothing while the moments ticked by.

"I know we don't have time for a proper honeymoon or trip or whatever," Isaiah began, his voice gruff without his nervousness. He wasn't entirely sure how Victor would take his suggestion, and he wasn't sure why he was making it, except that he didn't like how things were. He simply wanted to try to get to a better place before Victor left. "But if you want to go to the beach, we can go this weekend. I have a place, and Evan will be with Mick and Piper at that film festival thing…"

"I don't want to be any trouble," Victor said, trying to shift out of his arms, but Isaiah held him tight, needing to maintain the contact for a little while longer. Victor's voice when he spoke again communicated loud and clear that he didn't understand the mixed signal Isaiah was sending. "Isaiah, I don't get this. I don't know…"

"I want to do this for you. I don't want you to leave with it like this. I don't like this…" Isaiah released him and took two steps back to lean on the island as Victor turned around to face him. His husband's face was curious, not angry or defensive, but also open, which was very encouraging. "We started this better than where we are, right? I'd like to get back to that place."

Victor considered his words for a few long moments, his eyes scouring Isaiah's face for something, answers. Elusive goddamn answers. People rolled them out on TV like they came in the bottom of cereal boxes, but they didn't.

Victor bit his lip, his gaze flickering out to where his family laughed and talked around the table and then back again. His face was lit up with excitement, and Isaiah knew he'd gotten something right.

"Let's go to the beach."

Chapter Seventeen

The beach was gorgeous.

Mick and Piper had bundled Evan off for the film festival, Esther had gone back to her own house, and they'd packed a bag and jumped in Isaiah's truck and headed north to Oxnard. The drive was beautiful, relatively short, and totally worth it to get to see this view.

The house was small and modern, a split-level with an open concept living area on the top floor and the two bedrooms below. The light hardwood floors were everywhere, the furnishings all covered in shades of silvery gray and blue, and the entire back wall of the house was glass and looked out on the quiet beach and straight to the Pacific.

Victor dropped his bag on the floor and headed straight for the view, sliding back the door and stepping out on the deck. The wind ruffled his hair and brushed his skin, and he closed his eyes, letting the sounds of the birds and the waves and the smell of the salty air overwhelm his senses.

"I think you need to open your eyes to actually *see* the ocean," Isaiah said, his voice low and rumbling just beside his ear. The bulk of his body brushed along Victor's back, his breath ghosting along his cheek.

"I can see it," he answered, smiling into the breeze at Isaiah's huff of disbelief. "Shut up."

He felt Isaiah move away and opened his eyes, turning to find his husband leaning against the deck railing staring at him. His arms were crossed, and his expression was the usual serious contemplation Isaiah wore as a rule, but his eyes were softer, his sexy lips curved in an almost smile.

"You can't see the ocean staring at me," he said, suddenly confused by the atmosphere surrounding them. It was comfortable, easy, as if they now understood they could get back to where they'd begun. No matter how it happened, he was just happy to be there and not in the midst of whatever emo drama bullshit had haunted him the last few weeks.

"Have you never been to a beach?" Isaiah asked.

He shrugged, lifting his face to the bright sunlight and soaking in the best part of California and what he'd miss when he went back to the east coast.

"I'm usually working in a large city with little time to see the sights, and the beaches I've been to have been crowded and full of old men wearing speedos and topless grandmas." Victor winced, and Isaiah groaned and screwed up his face like he'd smelled something nasty. "Yeah, you can *never* unsee that."

"I didn't need to know that. Ever," Isaiah replied with a chuckle, pushing off from the deck railing. "Do you know how to surf?"

"A little." Victor considered his options and then shook his head. "I'd rather go for a run on the beach."

"Really?" Isaiah scrunched his nose and stared at him as if he'd sprouted a third eye.

"Really." And he couldn't explain it, but it was something he'd always wanted to do. "I thought this was *my* honeymoon."

Isaiah shrugged, rolling his eyes at what he still didn't understand. "Well, come on, then."

He followed Isaiah back into the house, grabbed their bags, and headed downstairs. He went into the room that was clearly for guests and changed his clothes. He met Isaiah in the kitchen, admiring how good he looked in his workout shorts, dark skin and muscles exposed and driving Victor crazy. He didn't know how easy it was going to be to run with a hard-on, but he'd try.

They took off down the beach, seagulls overhead and a line of luxury homes on the right. The weather was glorious, but the beach wasn't busy, the patrons of the private homes the only ones soaking up the rays and taking naps under large umbrellas. The sand gave underneath them, the waves lapping at their feet and getting their shoes wet, but they didn't care. They ran and joked and shoved each other in the surf, turning back when the sun started dipping down to the horizon, arriving back at the house when the sky was streaked purple and orange and navy blue.

"Last one in has to do the dishes!" Victor shouted as he kicked off his running shoes and socks and ran into the surf, diving into a wave just as Isaiah yelled behind him. He surfaced and looked around for his husband, kicking out when large hands wrapped around his ankle and pulled him under.

Victor slithered out from his grasp and turned on him, jumping on his back and hanging onto him like a monkey as they both broke the surface once again. Laughing and sputtering the little bit of water he'd taken in, Isaiah turned and faced him, arms and legs tangling as they floated, smiling.

"You cheated," Isaiah said, splashing him in the face. "I'm not doing the dishes. We won't be here long enough to clean up the mess you'll make if you cook."

"Asshole."

"Truth teller," he countered, coming in close enough to kiss, close enough for Victor to see the silvery droplets of water on his lashes. Isaiah leaned in, rubbing their noses and stubbled cheeks together before murmuring, "You're beautiful."

"And so soon he lies after saying he is an honest man."

Isaiah pulled back, looking down on him. His serious expression was back, his gaze intense even in the gloom of the evening. "Just take the compliment and let me feed you."

The pull of this man was dangerous, although he could fool himself that a little indulgence of touch, maybe a kiss or one more night together, wasn't really a problem because future distance would halt whatever was happening between them. He leaned in close, licking a salty droplet off his husband's lower lip. "Then feed me."

They swam to shore, grabbing their shoes and jogging for the deck illuminated by the interior lights. The house was gorgeous, the warm glow inviting, a siren's song that would entice sailors to risk crashing their ships on the rocks just for the chance to hear one note.

"Let's grab a shower and eat," Isaiah said, tossing his wet shoes on the deck and motioning for Victor to do the same just as a cell phone rang inside the house.

"That's Ian's ringtone," Victor said, picking up the device from the counter and looking to Isaiah with an eyebrow raised. "Should I answer or ignore?"

"Answer it. He'll keep calling, or call me looking for you," Isaiah said, moving around the island to the refrigerator. He opened it, reached inside, and emerged with two bottles in hand. "Beer?"

Victor nodded, swiping across the screen to take the call. "This better be good, Ian. I'm wet, cold, hungry, and thirsty."

"If that's Isaiah's idea of how to treat you on a romantic beach getaway then you should probably divorce him," Ian said, his clipped British accent wringing sarcasm out of every syllable. In typical Ian fashion, he didn't wait for Victor to respond. "I have news. New York has made you an offer. Principal dancer, the salary you wanted, and a two-year contract."

He sucked in a breath, his skin going even more chilled with the news. The reaction was peculiar considering it was exactly what he wanted—well, what he should do.

"That's...perfect." Victor looked up as Isaiah stood in front of him, holding out the cold bottle. He took it, taking a healthy gulp before signing off. "Thanks, Ian."

His agent and friend hung up with an "I'll send you the contract when I get it," and then the line was dead, and his future was decided.

Victor placed the phone on the counter and took another drink, looking everywhere but at the man standing in front of him smelling of seawater and sunshine and looking like every reason to hate the news he'd just received. Isaiah inserted himself in his line of sight, forcing the focus on him and the concern etched between his raised brows.

"What did he say?"

"I have an offer from New York." His voice was wooden even to his own ears, and the words stuck on the roof of his suddenly dry mouth. "Principal dancer. Two years."

Isaiah hesitated for only a moment, his body tense before he reached out and drew him into a tight hug. Victor wrapped his arms around him, returning the embrace and trying to center his emotions. They were all over the place when they should have been so clear.

Nothing had been clear since he'd met Isaiah.

His husband pulled back, the kiss pressed to his lips tender but intense, a combination of tongues and heated breaths and achingly potent grazes of teeth. Victor's senses were on high alert, tuned in to the rapid beat of Isaiah's heart, the goose bumps on his smooth skin, the firm pressure of his fingertips on his hips. He knew what was coming for them, but he was firmly rooted in the here and now.

Isaiah withdrew, his gaze locked on Victor's, the kiss only a whispered memory of the one they'd just shared.

"It sounds like we have something to celebrate."

Chapter Eighteen

He was dancing.

Isaiah stepped away from the kitchen island, tossing the dish towel on the counter as he finished up the last of the dinner dishes and peered through the windows out to the beach. The meal had been festive, both of them sticking to the celebration of the new job, avoiding the topics of moving and change and trips home to make it look good to the government. They didn't talk about expectations or the inevitability of other men in their beds or how it would eventually end. They didn't talk about activism or reporters or football teams. They didn't talk about Stephen or loss or how the past kept him from moving forward.

They'd stuck to the things that made them laugh and tease and flirt, pretending that this night was really the beginning of them—a honeymoon—and not the beginning of the end.

And now Victor was dancing in the moonlight.

Isaiah slid the door open and stepped out into the night. The deck lights had been turned off to allow the stars to shine, but the warm glow from the interior lights was enough for him to see his husband clearly.

He was beautiful.

All sinew and muscle and grace, he moved in a way that made it look effortless, but Isaiah knew better. Every jump, every twist, was executed with a precision that Victor spent several days per week perfecting, and the result was stunning. He moved like he heard the music in his head or in his soul. The result was powerful. So powerful that it rooted Isaiah to the spot, his chest pounding with the rapid thuds of his heart. What was it about Victor that spoke to him, that pulled him into his orbit and refused to let him go? He danced like he lived, as if he wasn't going to waste a moment of feeling everything, doing everything, throwing his entire being into the task of really living. It was captivating, confusing, because this mercurial, loud, brash man was nothing like the one he'd loved and married all those years ago. At one time Stephen had been everything he wanted and needed, and he'd filled every part of him with light and contentment. A quiet love that had grounded him.

Victor was as disruptive as a hurricane, not to the life he'd built for Evan; there Victor craved the stability of a home as much as anyone who'd never had it. No, the wrecking ball he wielded was aimed at Isaiah's heart, an organ that had barely made it through the last heartbreak. It was truth time here in the moonlight, standing on the deck of the home he'd shared with the man he'd loved, and the truth was that he was looking at a man he could love just as much — if he let go. And that scared him.

But he couldn't look away. Couldn't stop wanting him.

When Victor stopped, chest heaving with his effort, a sheen of sweat on his bare chest made him shine in the moonlight. He was just about the sexiest thing Isaiah had ever seen.

But this dance. It wasn't a seduction even though it had

him reeled in. It was melancholy, powerful, intense. The moves were agonized, the stops poised on a knife's edge, the arms not just flung open but empty, reaching for whatever had been ripped from its hold. His face was contorted in pain, a mask of mourning and grief that Isaiah recognized quite well.

This dance was painful to watch on one level, but unexpectedly hopeful and uplifting at the same time. The silence when it ended was unexpected, a strange revelation since there had never been any music to begin with, but Victor's talent made you feel the rhythm.

Isaiah clapped, descending the steps from the deck onto the sand. Victor's head whipped up from his final pose, surprise quickly overtaken by embarrassment. Isaiah grinned; he'd never seen this man shy or self-conscious about anything, and it was damn cute.

Actually, it was sexy as hell, and his body reacted to the half-naked man standing in front of him in the moonlight. He could still feel the touch of his skin on his palms and the taste of him on his tongue. As delicious and tempting as candy, and just as bad for him, when he knew he wouldn't be able to moderate his craving. It would be everything; it would be life changing. A risk of his heart, one he wasn't sure he was ready to make, but might not have a choice.

"How the fuck do you do that to me?" Isaiah asked when he stopped in front of Victor.

"Do what?" Victor ran his fingers through his hair, pushing the long strands off his face. He was still breathing heavily, but his smile was sweet and sexy with curiosity.

"*You* keep surprising me." He motioned around them where the sand was kicked up by Victor's dance. "What was that?"

"Something I'm working on for the New York event."

"It was stunning. Amazing," Isaiah said, his voice reverent and low. "You fucking blow me away."

"You *have* to say that." Victor shoved against his arm as he walked past him to get to the house.

Isaiah snagged his hand and pulled him back, slipping his arm around his waist and tipping him over into a low dip. Nobody was more shocked than Isaiah; he wasn't a dancer, but he just couldn't keep his hands off Victor tonight. Maybe it was the fact that he was leaving that compelled him to imprint the feel of him on his skin.

"I don't *have* to say anything," he answered, not letting go of Victor when he lifted back to a standing position. "But *you* have to dance with me."

His husband chuffed out a quick laugh, eyebrows scrunching together in confusion. "Now, *you're* surprising me."

"Just keeping you on your toes."

There was no music, and it really wasn't a dance, just the two of them swaying slowly in the moonlight. They were both still shirtless so the slide of bare skin on bare skin, slicked by the sea air and sweat, was delicious, and he just didn't want to give it up.

"How long have you had this place? It's wonderful," Victor asked, his voice barely a puff of air against Isaiah's cheek.

"It wasn't mine. It was Stephen's house. It had been in his family for years." He nuzzled into Victor's neck, loving the scratch of his scruff and swallowing down the dull ache that still hit him when he thought about the man he'd loved and lost. "When he passed, he left it to Evan. I'm taking care of it until he's old enough to have it."

"What a wonderful legacy," Victor murmured. "You must have amazing memories of this place."

"I do." He turned his head to look at his husband, Victor so close they exchanged breaths with every inhale and exhale. "We both do. It's all we have."

"Will I be a good memory, Isaiah?" His body was languid beside him, no doubt a combination of the alcohol and the sunshine loosening his limbs and his tongue, but Isaiah was in no better shape.

The words came easily in the gloom; the shadows covered up what he didn't want seen. "Yeah. You'll be a good memory."

"You'll be a good memory, too." Victor reached out a hand and traced his jawline with a finger, sliding it down to tangle their fingers together as he stepped out of the dance. He moved toward the steps, tugging Isaiah behind him. His words were low and almost lost in the breeze whipping up from the ocean, but Isaiah was so tuned in to him that he heard every word. Felt every word across his skin, in his electric nerve endings, in the heaviness of his cock.

"I'll be gone soon, and I don't want to waste the one night of our 'honeymoon' with regret and sad talk. You said you wanted us to get back to the way we began. I want that, too." He stopped at the top, turning to look down on Isaiah with a smile that was fierce and needy, brave and incredibly sexy. "I just want you to fuck me, and then I want to sleep with you all night. Can we do that?"

There was never a chance he was going to say no. He didn't want to waste time being pouty about their situation when he could just make great memories with Victor. And memories of their first night together made him smile and his dick get hard. Victor under the stars was the best kind of memory, and things had been easy between them. Nothing but two men and undeniable chemistry crackling between them.

He growled low in his throat and surged up the stairs to his husband who stepped back and chuckled with surprise. Isaiah lunged, shouldering Victor at the waist and hefting him over his shoulder in a modified fireman's carry. The benefit of being a football player: even though Victor was a big man, he could still bench press about five of him with no problem.

"Isaiah." Victor squirmed, his voice laced with laughter that ruined any chance he had at severity. "Put me down."

"I intend to," he said, dumping him on the two-person deck lounger with a bounce that made the wooden seat scrape the deck with a noise that would have drawn the attention of the neighbors if the constant crash of the ocean wasn't buffering the sound. "Get naked, stay put, and think of how much you're going to love sucking my cock."

He smiled at Victor's enthusiastic reaction in Russian as he headed into the house to grab the supplies he was now glad he'd decided to throw into his bag at the last minute. When he returned to the deck, he found his husband kneeling on the lounger, naked with his dick in his hand. The stroke up and down his shaft was slow and sensual, the wet, pink head a delicious visual treat that Isaiah could not resist.

Slipping off his shorts, he dropped to his knees in front of Victor, swallowing him down in one smooth move. He was hard, salty, silk over steel that filled his mouth. Isaiah slid up his length, swirling the tip with his tongue, a move that made his husband sway, locking his hands on Isaiah's shoulders for balance.

"Isaiah," Victor said, more of a breath than a word, and Isaiah loved the sound of his name on his lover's lips. Arousal made his accent thick, and the effect was something sexy and exotic.

Isaiah ran his hands over the muscles of Victor's thighs, the hair tickling his palms and then giving way to the smooth globes of his ass. He sucked on his shaft, his fingers parting Victor's cheeks to gently stroke the cleft and the tight ring of muscle of the entrance to his hole. His lover pushed back against his touch, alternately flexing his hips to fuck into Isaiah's mouth, hard and deep. The burn caused by Victor's cock stretching his mouth only added to how good this felt, and he gave in, letting Victor use him while his fingers rubbed and stroked his entrance.

There was an urgency in his movement, but Isaiah was in charge of this situation, or at least he was until Victor stopped and pulled his cock out of his mouth, looking down at Isaiah with blue eyes darkened with lust and hair mussed from the wind and his fingers. With the moon and stars behind him, Victor looked like a dark angel, but his sex-soaked voice made it clear that he was the devil in disguise.

"Do you want my ass or my mouth?" He reached out and cupped Isaiah's jaw, rubbing the pad of his thumb over his swollen bottom lip before dipping inside for him to taste and suck. "You can have anything you want. Just like that first night, I just want you."

"I want your ass, baby."

Simple question. Simple answer.

Isaiah rose up, gently pushing at Victor's hip to get him to lie back on the cushions. His lover complied, body open and relaxed, one arm placed behind his head to give him a direct view of Isaiah between his knees. He spilled lube over his fingers, slicking them up to make sure Victor would be ready for him, because it wouldn't be an easy ride. He wanted him, needed him, and gentle and easy wasn't happening the first round.

Isaiah pushed his legs wider, leaning over and taking Victor's cock in his mouth, as deep as he could take it while he trailed his hand down between his ass cheeks, spreading the lube over his hole. He massaged the opening, inserting a finger when Victor pushed down, working it in and out of his slick heat.

"More. Please," Victor begged, his moan and the writhing of his body making it hard to resist taking this too fast. But he wanted this to be good for his lover, wanted it to be a good memory.

He inserted another finger, stretching him open and then adding a third when he released Victor's dick from his mouth and eased up and over his body, sucking and biting and licking across his abdomen and torso. His nipples were dark against the pale light of his skin, tips hard against Isaiah's tongue as he sucked on them, loving the way Victor's panting breaths became needy and hungry, sounds that made Isaiah's dick impossibly hard.

"Isaiah," Victor gasped, his face partially hidden by the arm flung across it. His lips were swollen and red, teeth marks giving away his attempts to keep from Isaiah the sounds that were rightfully his.

"Look at me," Isaiah demanded, pulling his arm away and waiting until Victor focused his passion-glazed eyes on his own. "I'm going to fuck you, but you'll give me everything. No hiding your face or holding back your sounds. They're mine, and I want them. Do you understand?"

Victor nodded, his fingers digging into Isaiah's shoulders, pulling him down to him for a kiss. It was hungry and brutal, more teeth than soft lips, their bodes writhing against each other, chests and bellies slick with sweat and pre-come and lube.

"I need you to fuck me."

Isaiah shivered at the raw plea from his lover, remembering how they'd fucked before and how good it had been to have Victor deep inside him. The way his husband gave it all, pure hedonism and lust in his pleasure, totally shameless.

With shaky fingers, Isaiah slid on the condom and more lube and positioned himself between Victor's thighs, pressing inside tight, hot inch by inch. The first push all the way inside his lover was like a drug hitting his system, and he was craving more.

"Oh my God." Isaiah breathed out on a groan that sounded like it was ripped from his soul. "You're so tight, so good."

Victor wasn't a passive lover, his body moving to meet his with every thrust of his hips, fingers dragging along his chest, his biceps, his ass. He pulled him closer, lips skimming over sensitive skin and teeth leaving marks that he would feel for days. And all the time he was buried inside him, feeling like he was home after a long journey through the desert.

Isaiah leaned up and took Victor's mouth, tongues stroking and swirling, wet and messy and sloppy as they tried to consume each other. The tempo mirrored the pace of the fuck, hard and fast and desperate.

Isaiah needed to slow them down or this wouldn't last, and he needed it to last. Needed to be inside this man for as long as he could. He flipped them over, holding Victor tight against him until he straddled him from above, pale skin luminescent in the moonlight, the stars framing his beautiful body.

"Come on and ride me, baby. Show me how much you want me," he urged, snapping his hips upward and driving his cock deep inside his lover.

Victor arched his back, muscles rippling as he undulated over him, sliding up and down his shaft. It was a dance, a carnal, sexy movement of his body that he'd never forget. It would be etched on his mind, burned on his soul, and if he was lucky, the last memory that would pass his mind at the very end.

"You're so deep," Victor said in a voice coated with his own passion, his hunger and need. "So deep. Fuck, yes."

Isaiah ran his hands all over his skin, memorizing the flat planes of his abdomen, the silk of the fine hair on his arms, the dips and valleys of his hips. Victor's cock, long and thick, rode along his own belly, the head slick with his own arousal, and Isaiah reached down to palm it, stroking it in time with the rhythm of their bodies.

"You're so beautiful," he murmured, the words more of

a prayer than anything else. Victor looked down at him, eyes half hidden by his eyelids, lashes dark crescents against his pale skin.

He felt the clench of his lover's body around him before he saw his head loll backward, neck arched, as he cried out his pleasure and spilled over Isaiah's grip. He fucked up into his lover, hoping to draw out Victor's orgasm for as long as possible, but the movement of his hips, the way he rode him, had Isaiah following him over.

Isaiah trembled through the pleasure, shivering as goose bumps raced over his skin and pulses of electric shocks shot up his spine. He wrapped his arms around Victor's waist to pull him down and hold him close, heartbeat to racing heartbeat. He didn't want to let him go; so many things threatened to slide off his tongue when Victor buried his face against his throat and sighed heavily with contentment.

This was what he wanted. This is the man he needed. He didn't want Victor to go to New York. The knot of fear in his chest was there, still tight and suffocating, but he had to find a way to push past it, or he might lose everything.

"There are…" Isaiah licked his lips, finding his voice too rough to continue without swallowing hard. "There are things I think we need to talk about."

Victor shook his head, burying his face in the crook of his shoulder, his words were muffled against his skin, but Isaiah understood. "Not now. Not while we're both still coming down from the fuck of our lives and the fucking stars are making this the perfect movie moment." He took a deep breath and exhaled. "If you ask me anything right now, I'll do it. So don't. Not now."

Victor lifted his head and looked at Isaiah, and he was shocked at the vulnerability he saw there. It was raw and scary, and Isaiah had to force himself not to look away. They were both in deep and neither of them knew how they'd gotten there. The next step was the terrifying one, the one off the cliff into the dark. His lover was right…for now.

Isaiah pulled him close and kissed his mouth, his nose, his chin before shifting to lie down with him and stare at the stars. "I won't ask now, but I will soon."

Chapter Nineteen

The house was quiet with Evan at school.

The ride back from Oxnard in the early morning traffic had been quiet, words not coming easily to either of them. Neither awkward or wholly comfortable, it just…was. Now, back at the house, it all boiled down to flights and moving plans and a new kind of future—a future he wasn't embracing because it wasn't really what he wanted. That future was here in this house with Isaiah and Evan.

Last night had made that clear to him, and he knew it had been the same for Isaiah, but this move wasn't his to make. He was the outsider looking in on this family, and he couldn't invite himself in. He didn't regret shutting down whatever Isaiah had wanted to say last night, but now he was on pins and needles wondering when it would happen. So far his husband had been quiet, no outward indication that he wanted to discuss it in the harsh light of the morning.

"Thank you for last night, Isaiah," he said as they mounted the stairs side by side as they hurried to get their busy day started. On the landing in front of Isaiah's door, he turned to face the man he knew he was going to miss. The one he was going to regret leaving. "It was perfect. The house is gorgeous."

Isaiah opened his bedroom door, pausing to look at Victor with an expression that gave nothing away, especially not his conversation starter. "You said last night that you didn't want me to say things that we could have chalked up to the moonlight and amazing sex."

His mouth went impossibly dry, but Victor was able to force out his one word answer. "Yes."

"Well, I'm awake and sober and while I remember the amazing sex and hope to do it again, I don't think it's clouding my judgment."

"Okay." Victor huffed out a short laugh, mesmerized as Isaiah moved toward him and slid his bag off his shoulder.

"I've got to get to training, and you've got to get ready for your flight later, but I want to have that talk. I want to talk about you not going to New York if you can stay here in L.A. And I want to talk about changing the rules between us." Isaiah backed away from him, his gaze never leaving his own as he entered his bedroom with Victor following like he was the Pied Piper. Victor watched Isaiah as he took their bags and placed them side by side on the bed before reaching out and pulling him in to his body. "The first rule I'd like to change is where you sleep. You okay with that?"

For a guy who usually had a lot to say, the words were hard to find. "I'm okay with that."

"Good." Isaiah smiled and leaned down, pressing a soft kiss to his lips before pulling back and leaving Victor dazed and confused and happy. "We'll talk tonight, I promise."

The phone rang, and Victor hoped it was Isaiah.

He'd left the house when Victor was still in a daze, reeling from the turn of events and wondering how it had happened. Now he was trying to pack and organize for his trip to New York while checking his watch every five minutes.

He checked the caller ID and bit back disappointment that it wasn't his husband, but curious that it was Evan's school. He swiped the screen and answered the call, listening for a few moments before grabbing his keys and heading out the door.

He arrived at the school, a huge private institution that looked more like a fancy hotel than a place where teenagers spent their days learning algebra and history. But when the parents were celebrities and rich people, they weren't going to send their kids to an ugly building made of cinder block and painted a sickly green color.

He found Evan in the headmaster's office, bloody lip and black eye already swelling, with a butterfly bandage covering a cut on his right cheek. Evan's expression was miserable but also mutinous and belligerent, and Victor knew that whatever this was, it wasn't going to be easy to fix.

He walked over to his stepson and kneeled in front of him. "Are you okay? Did the school nurse check you out?"

Evan nodded, but his eyes took on a sheen of tears, and Victor pulled him close, wrapping him in a tight hug while the boy worked through his emotions. There was always an emotional aftermath to any physical fight, and Evan needed to let it out and then collect himself for the discussion they had to have. When Evan's hold loosened, he leaned back and took a good, long look at the boy who was so close to being a man. A good man.

"What happened?" he asked, wiping away a dash of leftover tears from Evan's cheek, turning when the door to the office opened with force. Isaiah stood in the doorway, expression thunderous, wearing his workout gear from the stadium. Victor stood and offered what he could. "He's fine. Bruised, but the school nurse took a look at him."

Isaiah nodded, but brushed past him, pulling Evan up out of the seat and into a tight hug as Victor and the headmaster watched. Even from this distance, Victor could see the tremble working its way through Isaiah's body as he came down from his own adrenaline rush.

"What happened here?" Isaiah asked when he released Evan and turned to face the headmaster. Mr. Traynor stepped back, his face flushing with his reaction to the bellowing voice of the very large man standing in his office. "I don't pay outrageous fees to this school to have my son involved in a fistfight."

"Mr. Blackwell, I'm sorry to tell you that Evan started the physical altercation, and because of that I have no choice but to suspend him for two days. The other boys will also be suspended," he added quickly, seeing the rage in Isaiah's expression. "We have a zero tolerance policy on violence."

"What's your policy on hate speech?" Evan asked, his voice loud but not quite at the level of yelling.

"Evan, watch your tone. I didn't raise you to treat the headmaster with disrespect," Isaiah warned, his glare now focusing on his son. The glare-off continued for several long moments, and Victor noticed the resemblance between the two of them. Evan might have been adopted, but the stubborn set of his jaw was 100 percent Isaiah Blackwell.

"He needs to show me some respect. In fact, this place needs to start showing all queer people a little respect! If they did, then I wouldn't have had to listen to those assholes and their hate." Evan was shouting now, and Victor knew that his adding cursing to the mix was not going to get Isaiah to listen. But the kid was on a roll, and nobody was going to speak until he'd had his say. "They called me a faggot and said that Victor should have been sent back to get gassed like all the homos."

The words hit him like a physical punch in the gut and very likely had the same impact on everyone else, since the room was so silent that Evan's hiccupy breaths sounded like the rev of an engine.

"I'm not going to be like you and sit by and do nothing while other gay men get beaten and laughed at or worse. I'm not going to be quiet, Dad. I'm going to fight like Victor, and I'll do it again to the next person who says such hateful things. I don't care if I get expelled, and if you try to stop me, then you're nothing but a coward who won't fight."

Victor was reeling. Pride warred with fear that Evan was taking on a fight when he didn't fully understand the consequences. And he never wanted to be the cause of a wedge between Isaiah and his son. "Evan, that's so brave, but you can't just…"

Whatever he was going to say died in his throat when Isaiah turned on him with eyes full of anger and body rigid with anger. His tone was icy, sending chills up and down Victor's spine.

"Keep out of this. It's family business."

"I thought I was part of the family," Victor stammered out, his voice full of emotions he was fighting back.

"That's where you're wrong." Isaiah's voice was loud and firm, but didn't hold even a hint of cruelty. He wasn't saying it to hurt him—it was just his truth.

He heard the gates clang as they shut down between them. The message was clear: he was on the outside.

"Dad!" Evan was furious, shoving against his father in anger, and Victor winced. He didn't want them to strike out at each other, not over him. "He is family. Don't be a jerk."

Isaiah turned on Evan, taking him by the arm and marching him toward the door. "Mr. Traynor, I need to use your office. Can you please wait outside with Evan?"

The demand was completely high-handed, but the man

scurried to comply, ushering the sputtering and angry Evan out of the door. With the door shut behind them, his husband focused his fury on him, and Victor braced for impact. This was going to hurt. He just knew it.

"All I ever asked you was to keep your shit away from Evan. I told you I didn't want him pulled into your activism, your nonstop Pride parade and protest march bullshit."

Isaiah was shaking with anger, and while Victor knew it was more about his being worried about Evan, it still cut him to the quick. How many times were they going to come back to this point? When would Isaiah accept that Victor was compelled to speak out and stand up? It wasn't a slight to him if he chose not to live out and proud, but it didn't give Isaiah the right to continually point out that his support of the things that were important to him was a problem.

"You need to get one thing straight, Isaiah. I didn't bring this to him. Life brought this to his door. He lives in this world where he's going to have to confront homophobic assholes who think people are less than human because of who they love. That's not me and my so-called protest bullshit, that's reality and, while I don't want him to get hurt, I'm proud of his courage and convictions. He's a great kid."

"He is a great kid and he deserves better than this. We, Stephen and I, *his family*, pulled him out of the system, away from violence and fighting, and gave him a life where he'd be safe." He slashed a hand at Victor, the ugliness in the gesture mirroring the venom in his tone and the unspeakable hurt inflicted by his words. "We worked damn hard to make sure he could grow up safe and happy. But you don't care about that. Fuck, I invite you into our life, and all you bring to the table is a bunch of ideas and causes that he can't possibly understand. And what's the result? Some kids call you a name and he gets suspended and a face that looks like he's been in a bar fight."

"I don't know what rock you're living under, but I didn't

bring this to his life." He motioned toward the door where Evan had exited a few moments before. "Have you taken a good look at your son? He's biracial, and half the time he wears dresses and makeup. Evan is an original, and he wants to experiment with gender, and he'll likely do the same with his sexuality one day. He's an artist and creative, and flamboyant and outspoken, and different. He's never going to be like anyone else and, while that difference is amazing, it's going to get him attention he may not want someday. Believe me, I know what I'm talking about."

"He's my son. You're not telling me anything I don't already know, but I also know that he idolizes you, and he never got in this kind of trouble until you came into our lives." Isaiah took a breath, the steadying gesture deceptively calm, because his next words cut down to the quick. "You say you care, but I have to wonder about that when you keep pushing him into these situations where he could get hurt."

"I do care! I would *never* put Evan in a situation where he could be hurt." Victor took a deep breath, incredulous that Isaiah could even think for a moment that he would endanger the boy he'd come to care so much about. "I love Evan. I love him just like I love you."

The silence in the room was not encouraging. The mask of withdrawal that descended over his face was devastating.

"That's not...we're not about that." He never even looked away. Isaiah maintained eye contact the entire time. How could you not believe a man who looked you in the eye and broke your heart?

"Love? We're not about love?" Victor asked, pushing the issue, pushing to get the answer that would penetrate his brain and finally drive the point home so he could stop reaching for the dream that some masochistic higher power kept dangling in front of him like a gold ring. "So what are we about, Isaiah?"

Isaiah considered him for a moment, and his hesitation to deal the killing blow was the only consolation for Victor. Somebody famous had said that when someone showed you who they were, then you should believe them. So when he sighed and delivered the final blow, he believed him.

"We're convenient, Victor, that's all."

Chapter Twenty

There was no silence more deafening than being ignored by a teenager.

Isaiah stood outside Evan's door listening for any signs of life. He'd taken his iPad, laptop, iPod, and cell phone. The boy had been completely cut off from the world for the two days of his suspension, and then he'd chosen to refuse to speak to the one person he was allowed to talk to.

He'd given him space to wallow in his anger, because Isaiah knew Evan was pissed, but now it was time to break the standoff and hash this out. He knocked on the door and waited, knocked again and waited. Nothing.

"Evan, I'm coming in because I'm the parent and I pay the mortgage on this house." He didn't wait; he'd given as much warning as he was going to give a fourteen-year-old kid.

Isaiah opened the door and scanned the gloomy room. The blinds were closed, and the result was an almost funereal vibe to the room. Clothes were all over the floor in piles, but that was the usual state of his room. Evan swore he knew where everything was and insisted on not allowing the use of the word "sloppy." He preferred "organized chaos," but from the looks of the room in the dim light, today it was just a mess.

Isaiah headed over to the lump lying under the covers in the dark and pulled back the covers at the head of the bed. Two huge boy feet were on the pillow. Gross. He flung the covers back over them, shielding his eyes from the sight, and went looking for the part of his son he wanted to talk to.

Evan grumbled when he pulled back the blanket and exposed his face. "Dad, too early."

"You've had two days to mope, but now we have to talk." Isaiah slid down to the floor and leaned back against the bed. At this level, he could see Evan's face clearly, and his heart sank when he saw the evidence of tears on his face.

"Is Victor coming back?" he asked, his voice growly from his sleep.

After their private talk in Mr. Traynor's office, Victor had left the school and, when Isaiah and Evan had returned after a visit to their doctor to make sure his injuries really were minor, they'd found him gone. He'd left a note explaining he'd been able to get an earlier flight, and he needed the extra rehearsal time for the New York event. That had been mostly a lie and they'd both known it. Evan had cast a mutinous glance in his direction and stomped off to his room, refusing to speak to him. Isaiah decided to table that discussion for now.

"We need to talk about why I grounded you even though I persuaded the headmaster to rescind your suspension," he said, hoping he could find the right words to explain his position on this. Once again, Stephen would have been better at this, but he'd do his best and hope that it got through to the son he was quickly realizing was a young man he didn't fully understand. "Violence is not the answer, Evan. You're too smart to be goaded into using your fists. Self-defense is one thing. If you get caught in a situation and you need to fight your way out to get to a safe place, then do it, but this…"

"But sometimes violence is the only answer left, Dad. After all the words have been said, sometimes you have to make your point with a beatdown."

Isaiah winced at his words as Evan sat up in the bed, his wild hair sticking out all over. If he looked real close he could still see that scared, suspicious boy they'd brought home from the foster home. It broke his heart again to think of all the years Evan had endured without them.

"When we brought you home, you had bruises and evidence of bones that had been broken and not set properly," he said, reaching out to trace a circular scar on his son's strong shoulder. An old cigarette burn that still turned his stomach. "Your dad and I promised each other that we would bring you home and protect you from all of that stuff. I won't let you create this kind of risk for yourself. I can't."

"Dad, that's a joke. Have you taken a look at me?"

He was confused. "I don't understand what you mean."

"Dad, really? Just being *me* creates risk!" Evan jumped off the bed, picking a dress off the floor and shaking it at him for emphasis. "I wear dresses and skirts and makeup. I'm skinny and not white, and my interests are fashion and photography and art." He dropped the dress and pointed at his chest, his hands shaking. "I'm queer, Dad. I like boys and girls, and it's not a shock to anyone, because there is no way I'll ever be able to pass."

"Pass? What are you talking about, Evan?"

"Pass, Dad. As a straight guy." Evan flung his hands out in a "what the fuck" as he continued. "I'll never be able to pass as a straight guy. I never have, and I never will. I'm not saying I want to, but yesterday wasn't the first time someone has called me a faggot or worse. It's not the first time someone has tried to kick my ass because they're a closet case and have to prove to their buddies that they don't want to kiss me." He pointed at himself again, his expression pleading for Isaiah to understand. "I'm just like Victor, Dad. We don't have to come out because we wear it on our skin. You're huge and athletic and a macho professional football player, and if you don't tell people you're gay, they never know, and even when you do tell them, they don't always believe you. If you wanted to, you could pass as straight. So, don't talk to me about me creating risk. I'm at risk because I can't hide who I am."

Isaiah was stunned, his mind reeling from what Evan had just shared. There was so much to process, but one thing jumped to the front of the line. "This has happened to you before?"

"Yeah, Dad," Evan said, slumping down into the desk chair across from him. "That school is just a mini world, and it has racists and homophobes just like the real world. I ignore them and then I try to talk to them and work it out, but sometimes that doesn't work, and I've had to fight my way out of it. This isn't the first time, it's just the first time I got caught."

"Evan." He knew his face was red from anger and embarrassment. "Why didn't you tell me?"

He shrugged. "It's what it is, and I was handling it."

"Getting into fights isn't the answer."

"It isn't my first choice." He sighed and pushed back in the chair, his handsome face scrunched up in concentration. "Look, it's like how you avoid driving in some parts of L.A. at night because you're a black guy. You know that the chance of getting pulled over is high, and being a rich and successful football player wouldn't help, so you just don't go there. But what if you had to do it? What if there was no other way to get home? You'd try to obey the laws and not get pulled over, but if you did, then the playbook would be completely optional. You'd do what you had to do." He shrugged again. "I *always* get pulled over, Dad, and while I don't go looking for a fight, if they bring it to me, then I'm not backing down. I have a voice, and I'm using it."

Isaiah groaned. He'd heard that before. "You sound like Victor."

"I take that as a compliment. He gets why I want to scream at the world sometimes." Evan smirked. "Okay, I want to scream all the time. And Victor is just like me. He doesn't stay quiet about things."

That stung. A direct hit to his heart. His words were petty and childish, and way too revealing about himself and his own insecurity. "You mean like me. I stay quiet."

"Dad, I'm not comparing you to Victor. You'd be the quiet, behind-the-scenes type even if you were straight. That's just you." Evan picked up his favorite lip gloss and waved it at him. "I'm just me, and he's just Victor. Loud and in your face. I love that about him, and I think it's what you love about him, too."

Isaiah stared at his kid, wondering how the hell they'd gone from discussing him getting in fights to this…loving Victor. He'd clearly lost control of the conversation and this situation, and he needed to rein it in and be the grown-up and do…grown-up things about it.

"We're not talking about Victor." Isaiah got to his feet and headed over to Evan, pulling him to his feet and into his arms for a huge hug. "I love you, kiddo. I'm proud of you and everything you are."

"I love you, too, Dad."

Evan snuggled into his shoulder and Isaiah smiled, remembering the first time Evan had allowed him to hold him like this. He'd been stiff with the residual fear of allowing someone too close, but it had been the best hug of Isaiah's life. Still was.

He released his son and turned to leave him to whatever the hell it was he did in here. He had some serious thinking to do over this situation with Evan. He'd thought they were close, and he still did, but there were things his son was dealing with that he'd never even thought about. That he needed to sink in and process so he could be a better father. This was a couple of steps in the right direction, to getting closer to each other.

"We need to talk about Victor, Dad. You need to apologize to him and tell him he's part of this family. This wasn't his fault, and you got all protective like you always do and said some really crappy things to him."

Isaiah sighed, stopped, and turned to face Evan who was sitting in the chair, looking like he wasn't going to let this go. So much for two steps closer; this discussion would probably insert a wedge between them. "Our situation is complicated."

"Well, duh. You married the guy to keep him safe. Nothing about this is normal, even I know that. I just don't understand why you pushed him away. We don't do that in this family."

"What do you mean?"

He rolled his eyes, typical teenager response to an adult clearly needing some sort of clue. "When Dad died, you told me that loving somebody was always worth it, even when losing them hurt more than anything in the world. You told me that when it comes to loving people being scared was never the acceptable answer. And even though I haven't psyched myself up to ask Benjamin Walls out yet, I'm going to."

"Wait." Isaiah put a hand up to stop him. "Who's Benjamin Walls?"

"He's this hot guy in my science class." Evan smiled, his ears turning pink with his embarrassment. "I think he likes me, but I'm not sure."

"He'd be crazy not to like you."

Evan shrugged. "You'd be crazy not to like Victor."

"I like Victor." He knew this was trap; the noose was tightening around him with every word he spoke.

"No, you *love him*, Dad, and he loves you, too. Even I can see the goofy way you two look at each other. It's kinda gross."

"It's complicated, Evan."

"Stop being afraid, Dad. We don't do that in this family." Evan crossed the room and stood in front of him, wrapping his arms around his middle to give him another hug. Isaiah held him close, ears tuned to whatever his son had to say about this. "I miss him. He fits with us, and he needs us."

Oh shit. Isaiah shut his eyes and hugged his son tight. It was like hearing Stephen and the countless conversations they'd had about petitioning to adopt Evan. He hadn't been the one to come up with the idea of adoption; he wasn't even sure he wanted kids. But Stephen had met Evan through a program at the college where he taught, and the kid had stolen his heart from that moment on. Stephen had eaten, breathed, and slept adoption for a year, and one day after a discouraging meeting with the judge, Isaiah had looked at a distraught Stephen and asked one simple question: "why are we doing this?"

Stephen had simply answered, "He needs us. We need to get him and bring him home."

And the moment Evan had slipped his little hand in Isaiah's, he'd needed this little boy.

And now he needed Victor just as much as Victor needed him, needed them.

It wasn't a lightning strike or a revelation sent down from the Almighty. No, it was so quiet that he'd almost missed the voice in his head that said, "I need him."

So, it was simple once again. He was going to go get him and bring him home.

Chapter Twenty-One

"Are you going to sign with New York or Los Angeles, Victor?"

Ian was sitting on the couch, papers spread all over the table in front of him while he punched numbers into a calculator. Victor watched him enter numbers on one of his countless spreadsheets and flip between the papers before looking up at him with a serious expression on his face. They were talking about money, and Ian was always serious about money.

"If you look at only the numbers, the New York deal is more money in your pocket. The salary is higher, and you get bonuses for touring. They are dying to get you signed and roll out the red carpet."

"And Los Angeles?" Victor asked, turning back to the mirror to check his makeup. This afternoon he'd participated in a photo shoot, and the makeup artist had done a good job. Reporters from every major news source had been there, and he'd answered numerous questions about the work he was doing to raise awareness about the human rights violations occurring in his home country. He'd been very busy since arriving in New York, and he liked it that way. It didn't leave much time to think about Isaiah. "How do the numbers work for them?"

"No bonus for touring, but the base salary is better." Ian tapped on the screen and turned it toward Victor, displaying columns and data he didn't understand. "In the end, they're even. Just pick the place you want to be, and live the dream."

Victor scoffed, leaning forward to check his eyeliner. "No dreaming for me. I needed to wake up."

Ian sighed and shut the computer, throwing himself back onto the couch in a heap of designer suit and paperwork. He'd more than earned his fifteen percent, making last-minute travel arrangements when Victor had needed to get out of L.A. and coming with him when he'd figured out what a mess he was. Above and beyond, that's what Ian had delivered these past couple of days.

"Does Isaiah know about the offer from Los Angeles?" Ian asked, picking up his coffee and wincing when he took a sip of the cold brew. He stood up and walked over to the sink in the corner of room and dumped the cold liquid, popping a new cup into the machine to brew a fresh one. He looked back at Victor when he didn't answer. "I'll take your silence as a no."

"It will do no good to tell him. The best thing I can do for Isaiah and his family is to move to New York."

"Uh-huh. That sounds like bullshit to me." Ian poured his coffee and took a sip. "Or it sounds like Isaiah. Both sound alike sometimes."

"He's your best friend."

"Well, he's *your* husband."

There was no arguing with that statement, even though it was clearly in name only and would be until they didn't need to be married anymore.

"I didn't tell him." Victor stood up and moved toward where his costume hung on the rack, peeling off his sweats and underwear, and pulling on the flesh-colored leggings he'd wear for the performance.

He examined his reflection in the mirror; the dark shadows under his eyes were noticeable in contrast to the paleness of his skin. He hadn't slept on the plane, too wound up from the fight with Isaiah, and he never really rested in a strange hotel bed. And he'd missed Isaiah, warm and solid and wrapped around him from behind, big arms holding onto him like he was a lifeline. Victor had never had anyone need him like that, and it was addictive, something he'd have to get over with time.

And distance.

"I think I should take the New York job." Victor snuck a glance at Ian, gauging his reaction.

"I didn't take you for a runner, Victor."

Victor shook his head, not willing to take the bait. "I grew up in the custody of the state, little more than a work camp, and I got my ass kicked by people a lot scarier than you."

"Scarier than me?"

"Yes," he answered. "And they had Russian accents. So much scarier than your posh British one. You sound like the queen."

"The quee—" Ian paused, lifting his cup to his mouth, middle finger extended toward Victor. "Fuck you."

"Keep talking to me like that and I'll dock your commission to ten percent," Victor replied, moving to the middle of the room to do some light stretches to warm up his muscles. A glance at the clock informed him that he had a little under an hour to get ready for the performance.

"Are you nervous?" Ian asked, settling back on the couch and gathering up his papers. "Do you even get nervous anymore? Did you ever?"

"Yes, of course I do. I give a shit about it, so I get nervous," Victor answered, bending over at the waist and touching the floor with the backs of his hands, letting gravity loosen his body. "I get nervous every single fucking time."

"But you still do it, yeah?"

"Of course, it's my job." He paused, correcting his answer to be more honest. "It's my life. My heartbeat. My best friend. It kept me going when I had nothing."

"You love it." Ian sorted a stack of papers, looking through them before placing them in his briefcase. Victor stopped his movement, feeling the trap coming, but not sure from which direction it would come. He was going to pay for the crack about the queen, he could feel it. "You love Isaiah, too."

Oh, there it was. A shot to the heart.

He rolled up, flopping back into his chair, staring at the ceiling. "Do you know how weird this is coming from the guy who told me that his idea of a long-term relationship is fucking the same guy for a long holiday weekend?"

"I said it counted if it was a long weekend spent in an expensive hotel. If I'm not paying, then it's just casual."

"You just made my point," Victor said, rolling his head to the side to observe Ian at an angle. "Don't talk to me about love."

"I have a theory that those of us who are incapable of the emotion are the ones who see it clearly."

Victor didn't want to be interested, but he was. Still desperate for even a glimmer of hope. He was an idiot, but he was an idiot who wanted to hear what Ian had to say, because he wasn't ready to give up yet.

"Okay, Shakespeare, tell me what you see."

Ian shoved the last of his papers into his case and closed it with a metallic snap before easing back onto the couch cushions and giving him a long, serious look.

"Let me tell you a story." He smirked, clearly enjoying

this moment more than he should, and it was starting to piss Victor off, but not enough to get up and leave. "There were two princes who met, and they were hot together. Supernova hot." He winked at Victor with a knowing grin. "I was there so I can swear that it's true. Anyway, one prince had everything and lost it, and the other prince had nothing but was willing to fight for the right to have it." He held a hand up when Victor sat up a little straighter in his chair. "They recognized each other, the real person underneath their outward success and personas, and ended up married, but both were too scared to go after what they really wanted from each other. One prince was willing to shout from the rooftops about what he believed in, and the other lived quietly, the best revenge on those who think you don't deserve your happiness. They were two of the best princes out there, but they were both too scared to risk it all and fucked it up. The end."

"The end? You've seen the future?" Victor asked.

"You tell me, have I?"

A knock at the door interrupted them, the stage manager's face appearing in the crack of the door. She was in her mid-thirties, very nice, but Victor suspected she would rip his balls off if he was late and fucked up her schedule. She smiled at him.

"Cindy will come back to get you in about twenty minutes. Mr. Grayson from the AIDS Alliance will do your introduction, kind of like at the Kennedy Center Honors, and then you'll give your performance. Afterward, please stay on the stage, and Mr. Grayson will come out to give you the Alliance Award for Activism, and then you'll both exit stage right. Sound good? Any questions?"

"No. It all makes perfect sense, thank you," he responded, smiling at her as she nodded to them both and closed the door as she left.

He shifted in his chair, intending to do some last-minute

costume and makeup checks when Ian's voice reminded him that he was still there.

"You didn't answer my question."

It took a minute to refocus on what they'd been talking about; he was shifting into performance mode where nothing broke through but the music and the steps. It was his zone, his happy place. But he could answer his question, because this story, his story, he knew how it was going to end.

"You left some crucial facts out of your tale, so let me tell you a story. There were two guys, one a prince and one a pauper." Ian scoffed at this with a derisive snort and a wave of his hand in dismissal. "And they were hot together, molten lava hot. The prince had lost everything, but was still kind and loving and just about the sexiest thing the pauper had ever seen. The prince was also a great father and son, and he offered to help the pauper out when he was going to be thrown out of the kingdom. The prince was clear this rescue didn't come with emotional strings; the pauper would live in the castle, but he would not be royalty. The pauper wanted that to change, he fell in love with the prince and his family, and thought that maybe he would finally have the home he'd been searching for his entire life. He wanted to be with the prince in the castle and live happily ever after, and he thought the prince wanted that as well, but he was wrong. The prince just wants to live with his family in his castle, that's his happily ever after. The end."

Ian held up his hands, shaking his head as he got to his feet. "No. No. That's not the end of the story, you didn't tell me what happens to the pauper. Does he stay in the castle? What about his happy ending?"

Now it was Victor's turn to shake his head. Wasn't it obvious how this was going to end? "The pauper moves to a new kingdom and starts over with the fresh start the prince gave him. The end."

Ian observed him, his eyes searching, curious. He opened his mouth to argue, if the narrowing of his eyes was a true indicator of his mood, but then he shut his mouth and shrugged. "We'll sign the contracts for New York after the performance tonight."

The sooner he could write another ending, the better.

Chapter Twenty-Two

Getting past the stage manager took a phone call to Ian.

Appearing at the side staff entrance, Ian looked him up and down with a smirk that could have meant anything from "it's about time" to "you're an asshole." Actually, it probably meant both.

Proving once again what a true best friend he was, Ian glanced at the security guard and moved to close the door. "I have no idea who this guy is."

The guard cut him a weird look and answered, "Dude, he's Isaiah Blackwell. He plays football in L.A."

"I'm a rugby man myself," Ian continued, obviously enjoying this moment of humor at Isaiah's expense.

"Ian, don't be a dick. I need to see him." He waffled between glaring at him and pleading with his eyes, but finally decided to go for broke and beg. "Look, I messed up, man. Please, help me out."

His best friend gave him a long, serious look, but finally shoved open the door wide enough for him to walk through. He smacked Isaiah on the back of the head as he passed, hissing, "It's about fucking time, you dumb-ass."

"Where is he?" Isaiah rubbed the back of his head and dropped his overnight bag on the ground at his feet. "I need to see Victor."

He started walking toward the backstage area, presuming that it was in the direction of all the people, voices, and bustle. All he needed was five minutes with his husband, five minutes to tell him he loved him and see if he'd messed up so badly that he wasn't going to get a second chance.

Ian's long stride caught up with him, and he turned to block his progress, walking backward as he gave Isaiah the evil eyeball. "You can't bother him now. He goes on in a few minutes."

"Did he sign the contract with New York?" he asked, navigating himself and Ian around the obstacles of performers, costumes, and props as they headed toward the main attraction. At this question, Ian's face went blank and he turned in mid-step, effectively blocking Isaiah from seeing any part of his reaction.

He followed close on his heels, coming to a halt in an area just to the right of the stage. From the side, he could see performers currently on the stage, the rapt audience just beyond the stage lights. It looked like a full house, which was great news for the charity, but not so great for him if he pulled this off the way he wanted.

Isaiah tugged on Ian's arm. "Where is he?"

His friend nodded directly across the stage. At first, he couldn't see anything except bodies moving everywhere, some with headsets and clipboards, others just waiting for whatever cue they needed to spring into action.

And then he saw Victor.

Tall and steady, his dark hair falling over his forehead in a messy wave which was in contrast with his serene demeanor. It was as if nothing could touch him there, he was so focused on the performance ahead of him. There was no way he could interrupt him now, so Isaiah just drank him in slowly. And it was as if he was dying of thirst; he needed him that much.

Victor moved, shuffling out of the way of a man with a prop, and Isaiah got a look at his costume and almost dropped to his knees. Shirtless, pale skin glowing under the harsh lights, his only clothing was a pair of nude, skintight leggings. Every muscle, every ripple of smooth, taut skin was available for anyone to ogle. The hot flare of jealousy in his gut was eclipsed only by the deep sense of longing that shot through his veins and thudded into his pounding heart.

He loved him. Needed him. Wanted him.

There was no denying it. Victor was his, and he was Victor's.

"Has he signed the contract with New York yet?" Isaiah asked again, not taking his eyes off Victor.

Ian shifted beside him, and Isaiah could feel his hesitation. "If I tell you that, I'll violate client confidentiality."

"Ian." His voice was pitched low, but his friend couldn't miss the warning. Isaiah wasn't in the mood to fuck around on this.

Ian sighed. "No, he didn't." A brief pause and then Ian added, "Or the one from Los Angeles."

Isaiah turned to look at him then, not sure if he was pissed or excited. "Why didn't he tell me?"

"Why would he?" Ian replied, his eyebrow raised and eyes rolling. "Look, Isaiah, if you're just here to fuck with his head or give him some bullshit about the two of you not being in love, then just don't. He's made his choice. Let him have it."

"What did he choose?"

"New York. Because he thinks you don't want him."

Isaiah flinched. "Did he tell you that?"

"He didn't have to. You've been running scared on this since you saw him at the ballet that first night." Ian reached out and grasped his arm, pulling him out of the way of a man and young woman who approached them. Ian gestured toward the man. "Mr. Grayson, this is Isaiah Blackwell, Victor's husband." They shook hands while Ian explained further. "Mr. Grayson is making the introduction and giving Victor his Alliance medal."

"Unless you want to do it?" Mr. Grayson asked, holding out a piece of paper to Isaiah with a broad smile. "I understood you wouldn't be here, but it would be so much more meaningful if you gave it to him. And it would be quite a great surprise for the guests. We have many football fans here. The speech is written out and the process is simple: you introduce him, he dances, and then you give him the medal."

Ian snickered. "Isaiah doesn't like to give speeches."

He didn't. He didn't even like Q&A at postgame press conferences. But this… He would do this.

"I'll do it." He would have laughed at Ian's expression of shock if he hadn't had to swallow down the rise of panic in his belly. He was glad he didn't have much time to think about this or he'd find a way to back out or make himself nuts with the dread. "Give me the speech."

Mr. Grayson handed it over with a big smile and the plans of how to spin this to the benefit of the Alliance. Isaiah read it over, steadying his breathing as he familiarized himself with the words he'd just committed himself to saying in front of a packed concert hall full of people who'd paid a lot of money to be here.

"Masiello isn't going to like this," Ian murmured, his tone goading.

Isaiah paused, considered it, and decided he didn't care. "He'll get over it."

"Just breathe," Ian said, his hand on his shoulder. "Victor will hear you."

And that was really all that mattered.

Within a few whirlwind moments, the previous performer received their recognition and filed off the stage in a flurry of applause. And then it was quiet, and Ian's hand shoved him toward the podium.

Isaiah walked forward, squinting against the glare of the lights when he stepped onto the stage. The faces in the audience disappeared from his sight, but he waited a few seconds for the adjustment, and the first face he saw was Victor's. Shocked, conflicted, and beautiful; it was all he needed to see for courage, to do this thing for Victor.

He smiled at his husband and walked to the podium, spreading the typewritten speech out on the surface. Isaiah reviewed the words again, licked his lips, and looked up at the crowd spread out before him.

"Good evening. I'm Isaiah Blackwell, and I have the great honor of introducing Victor Aleksandrov, my husband."

The audience clapped, and he waited them out, using the time to glance down at the paper and calm his nerves. The speech was nice, complimentary, but it wasn't what he wanted to say; it wasn't what he wanted Victor and the world to hear.

"Tonight's performance is in honor of not only all the wonderful work the Alliance has done but to celebrate the work that Victor has only just begun on behalf of queer men and women everywhere who are the victims of human rights violations because of who they love." He took a breath, praying that he got the next part right. He might not get a second chance. "I'm a gay man, and I have been blessed to have loved and to be loved by two of the best men I have ever known. One was taken in an accident far too soon, and one entered my life completely by accident. The best kind of accident. I'm not an activist. I don't march in parades or make speeches—in fact, this one right here is killing me."

Laughter rippled through the crowd, and he took the chance to glance over at Victor, their gazes clashing across the distance. Victor had moved closer to the performance area, his face fully in the lights shining down on the stage so Isaiah could see his full expression, and what he saw there encouraged him to continue, to be honest and unafraid.

"I'm a quiet person, a private person, but Victor isn't, and the world is better for it. He's loud and disruptive and challenging and infuriating, and the messiest cook on the planet. He uses his talent and his voice to speak out against the atrocities in his country and in other countries, and his absolute refusal to keep quiet risked his own life and made it impossible for him to return home." Isaiah smiled. "Their loss was my gain because I simply don't know what I'd do without him. To watch him dance is breathtaking. To hear him speak is uplifting. To observe him playing video games on the couch with our son is joyful. To have him smile at me is...a gift. To have him love me is priceless. To love him is humbling and something I don't deserve."

Isaiah caught the movement from the corner of his eye, and he turned in time to catch Victor in his arms and respond to the kiss pressed to his lips. It was sweet and wet, and maybe just a little too "Rated R" for this crowd, but he didn't give a shit. Victor was kissing him, his warm, hard body pressed against him, and everyone else could wait five or ten until he got his world back in order.

Victor backed out of the kiss, his smile making Isaiah's heart do a flip. "You're an idiot."

"I am. I'm also sorry, Victor. Come home with me, baby, and let's be a family. Mess up the kitchen and leave your dance clothes all over the floor and sleep with me every night." He kissed him again, smiling into it when Victor laughed. "I love you."

"I love you, too."

"And?"

"I'd love to go home with you and be a family."

He kissed him again, long and deep because he could. He'd spend the rest of his life kissing his husband as often as he could. Isaiah looked around, nodding toward the audience watching the extra show. "So, how about you dance and I give you your medal and then we take the first flight back to Los Angeles?"

Victor smiled again, and it was like he'd won the goddamn Super Bowl.

But he could make it even better.

"And when we get home, I'm going to ask you to marry me again and you're going to say yes and we're going to let Evan and my mother plan the entire thing. Sound good?"

"Did I ever tell you that I could never say no to a Blackwell man?"

Isaiah kissed him one more time. "I hope you know that I will shamelessly use that to my advantage."

"For how long?"

"For the rest of my life."

Epilogue

Several months later

This time they were surrounded by family and friends.

Isaiah stood at the edge of their pool under the late afternoon sun with the man who'd entered his life so unexpectedly and then turned it upside down in the best way possible. Evan stood by them, beaming and holding the rings that would make them husband and husband…again.

They wore matching beige linen suits chosen by Victor and Evan for the ceremony and the pictures, but he'd picked out the matching board shorts they would change into for the pool-party reception. His mother had commandeered the food, and there was enough to feed all the guests and his entire football team and Victor's ballet company. The honeymoon would wait until football season was over, but two weeks on the pristine beaches of Tahiti would be worth the wait. Tonight they would head to Oxnard for a few days of sand and surf and sex.

It didn't matter; as long as they were together, it was the

best place on earth.

Victor reached out, taking his hand, and they turned to Ian. Newly ordained by an internet church, he had insisted on doing the honors, despite his own personal aversion to matrimony. Victor had joked that Ian was secretly a hopeless romantic, but he'd never made that mistake in front of Ian.

"Everyone, we're here today to join Isaiah and Victor in matrimony…again." Ian paused while the crowd clapped and whistled and yelled out their support. "They've requested that I keep this simple, but some things need to be said about these two men. Both strong and loving and kind, they care for their friends and family and each other in a way we should all emulate. They are both survivors. Both have endured pain and heartbreak and difficult times to reach this point where they both have embraced this second chance at happiness."

Ian smiled at them both, reaching out to lay his hand on the ones they had joined. "It's easy to love the first time, but it takes courage to love the second time after you've experienced the joy and pain of life. The way they love is an inspiration to all of us." One last smile and a squeeze before he let go and reached for the vows he'd printed out for the ceremony. "So, are you ready?"

Isaiah looked at Victor and grinned, his heart thudding with all the love he had for this man. His husband squeezed his hand and gave him a slow wink, promising something fun and wicked after the party was over and for the rest of their lives. Life with Victor was going to be unexpected and loud, and sometimes a test of wills, but they'd do it together.

He glanced at Ian, nodding for him to continue.

"We're ready."

Acknowledgments

Thank you to those who have inspired and encouraged me in writing this book: Josh Lanyon, Harper Fox, Hank Edwards, Rhys Ford, Jordan Castillo Price, Annabeth Albert, Karen Stivali, Santino Hassell, Megan Erickson, Heidi Cullinan, Damon Suede, Charlie Cochet, Jay Northcote, Garrett Leigh, Cat Sebastian, Z.A. Maxfield, and Amy Jo Cousins. Thank you so much. xoxoxo

About the Author

A *USA Today* bestseller, Robin Covington loves to explore the theme of fooling around and falling in love in her books. Her stories burn up the sheets…one page at a time. When she's not writing she's collecting tasty man candy, indulging in a little comic book geek love, hoarding red nail polish, and stalking Chris Evans.

A 2016 RITA® Award finalist, Robin's books have won the National Reader's Choice and Golden Leaf Awards and finaled in the Romantic Times Reviewer's Choice and the Book Seller's Best.

She lives in Maryland with her handsome husband, her two brilliant children (they get it from her, of course!), and her beloved furbabies, Dutch and Dixie Joan Wilder (Yes—THE Joan Wilder)

Drop her a line at robin@robincovingtonromance.com—she always writes back.

69 MILLION THINGS I HATE ABOUT YOU
a *Winning the Billionaire* novel by Kira Archer

After Kiersten wins sixty-nine million dollars in the lotto, she has more than enough money to quit working for her impossibly demanding boss. But where's the fun in that? When billionaire Cole Harrington finds out about the office pool betting on how long it'll take him to fire his usually agreeable assistant, he decides to spice things up and see how far he can push her until she quits. But the bet sparks a new dynamic between them, and they cross that fine line between hate and love.

TIED TO TROUBLE
a *Gamers* novel by Megan Erickson

When Chad Lake spots a sexy nerd at his sister's party, he can't resist trying to ruffle the guy's bow tie. But in the end, it's Chad who's left wide-eyed, his ears still ringing with the filthy things the guy whispered in his ear. Owen's heard *all* about the cocky Adonis, and he has every intention of steering clear of the man—until Chad's sexy taunts push him too far. There's something intriguing about Chad, though, and even though Owen knows the infuriating man is trouble, he can't seem to stay away...

His Heart's Revenge
a *49th Floor* novel by Jenny Holiday

A CEO in his own right, Cary Bell is competing for a major client with his boyhood crush. He's never forgiven himself for betraying Alex Evangalista. But with his professional reputation on the line, he's going to have to find his inner cutthroat if he wants his new company to succeed. Alex isn't about to let his nemesis steal a client out from under him. It's time to break Cary's company—and his heart.

The Billionaire in Her Bed
a *Worthington Family* novel by Regina Kyle

Real estate mogul Eli Ward knows he has a fight on his hands with his latest project. He doesn't expect that fight to be led by Brooke Worthington, the woman who rocked his world one unforgettable night. The one woman who doesn't know who he is, which is a good thing. Graphic designer and part-time bartender Brooke Worthington refuses to follow her family's plan for her. She's too busy building her artistic career. She doesn't have time for relationships, either, because she has to save the building she lives in from some greedy real estate billionaire.